The Mourning Trail

Book 2 of

The VIKINGS! Trilogy

Jay Palmer

ISBN-13:978-0-9911127-1-5

ISBN-10:0991112717

**

All Books by Jay Palmer:

The VIKINGS! Trilogy:

DeathQuest
The Mourning Trail
Quest for Valhalla

The EGYPTIANS! Trilogy:

SoulQuest
Song of the Sphinx
Quest for Osiris

The Grotesquerie Games

The Grotesquerie Gambit

The Magic of Play

The Heart of Play

Viking Son

Viking Daughter

More Books by Jay Palmer:

Jeremy Wrecker – Pirate of Land and Sea

The Seneschal

Dracula – Deathless Desire

Souls of Steam

Website: **JayPalmerBooks.com**

Cover Artist: **Brooke Gillette**

DEDICATION

To my three oldest and best friends:
Dave Dawes, Greg Greer, and Mike Brown.

Chapter 1

Torment

ELOISE

"Untie me, you bastards ...!"

Eloise clenched her teeth against the stinging in her throat, her shrill, raspy voice raw from screaming threats and curses, young eyes red and tearing. The Earls' tent, dark, stained canvas walls, stared silently back, illuminated only by glows from torches outside. Stout leather thongs bit deeply into her wrists and ankles, binding her, yet her sufferings were irrelevant.

Struggling was useless; Eloise's wrists had been bound behind her for hours, lashed to Seren's wrists. The older woman's dead weight pulled against Eloise as

Seren hung unconscious, both bound to their chairs with sturdy ropes and leather thongs.

Seren had quickly lost her voice; before passing out from exhaustion, she could only whimper and croak like a frog. Eloise had screamed with each crack of the whip, and sobbed when either Rafe or Karl cried out.

Earl Sir Guldwin had been merciless; he'd staked Karl and Rafe just outside of their pavilion, where Eloise and Seren had been ordered, and could hear him demand to know where his daughter and the Seer were hiding. Rafe and Karl swore they didn't know where they were, yet that didn't satisfy Earl Sir Guldwin. He ordered them both to be lashed to death.

Eloise had stormed out, shouting at Earl Sir Guldwin, cursing his name, his honor, and his chivalry before all his retainers. Seren, who'd followed Eloise out of their prison tent, had been grabbed and held back by surprised guards, yet had cursed them with a tongue to shame foul-mouthed sailors.

Earl Sir Guldwin gave Eloise all the respect he'd shown Roselyn: he backhanded Eloise to the ground. Seren screamed as Eloise fell, yet the old whore's struggles against the strong Saxon guards were vain.

More shocked than hurt, Eloise glared up at Sir Guldwin with a hate she'd never known, which paled even the darkness she felt for her despised stepfather. *Someday,* Eloise promised herself, *someday she'd kill Earl Sir Guldwin.*

Standing with all the poise and dignity of a baroness, Eloise faced Sir Guldwin. He was horrible, a despicable man with more ambition than any amount of power could satisfy. She stood helpless before him, a child against a commander of armies, yet she couldn't endure her friends being tortured.

"Take my barony," Eloise offered. "All of du Harmonn ... for a price."

"No ...!" Rafe cried, but a guard elbowed him hard in the stomach. Rafe collapsed, coughing, hanging between the two thick posts his wrists were tied to.

Although her stomach knotted, Eloise bit her lip and struggled not to react; she had to maintain self-control or her friends would suffer far worse. She glanced at Karl, who was tied between the posts next to Rafe; all their lives depended on her. Karl looked haggard, shirtless, bereft of his protective mail, yet still defiant. Their eyes met, and no words were needed; he was obviously worried, but calm, giving her a clear, reassuring glance. Eloise understood; Karl had confidence in her; he trusted her as much as she trusted him. Yet some other pain shadowed his eyes, an emptiness she'd never seen before.

"I already own your barony," Sir Guldwin snapped at Eloise, "because I own you." Then he hesitated. "What price ...?"

"Let us go," Eloise said. "Release me and my servant, and these two guards. Let us walk out of here, without pursuit, and quit looking for your daughter, the Druid, and our Viking friend."

"Your Viking friend is dead," Sir Guldwin said.

Eloise staggered. She almost fell, and only barely managed to keep standing. *Eric ... dead?* Implications faded before the blackness that rose and engulfed her. Eric was her confidant, the strongest man she'd ever known, and she hadn't even known he'd died.

For a moment, Eloise foundered, but then she stiffened and faced the Earl. Eric was gone, but her friends still needed her.

"Our freedom for my barony," Eloise said.

"Only the king can grant baronies," Sir Guldwin sneered. "Marriage to my son will give me hereditary ownership, and that I will have. You'll be an obedient wife and bear me many grandsons ... or I'll vivisect your friends before your eyes."

Earl Sir Guldwin smiled, a twisted, half-snarling smirk, reeking of arrogance and contempt. Behind him stood his retainers, old, thick-bearded, expressions ranging from serious to jovial. They were toying with her, and there wasn't anything Eloise could do. Behind the Earl's friends and kinsmen stood dozens of guards and servants, and they were in the midst of a huge army camp, with thousands of soldiers celebrating their victory over the hated Vikings and the death of King Svenson Two-Sword.

Eloise felt overwhelmed, yet tried not to show it; as bad as Sir Guldwin was, she'd faced worse.

"A forced marriage will forever taint your ownership and reputation," Eloise said. "Let my friends go free, all of them, and I'll marry your son willingly."

Sir Guldwin paused, scratched his trimmed beard, and stared at her.

"Now that is a worthy offer," he said. "Perhaps, if you made that offer with a less haughty tone, I might accept."

Eloise strained for control. To debase herself before this foul monster was unthinkable; dignity rebelled against the idea. Then Eloise glanced at Karl ... and the guards holding braided leather whips.

Slowly she bowed to the Earl, performed a perfect curtsey, and knelt before him upon the grass.

"My life and my barony ... for the lives of my friends," Eloise offered. "All I have ... for all I care for."

"Is that the best you can do?" Sir Guldwin laughed, and he crossed his arms over his chest. "My future daughter-in-law needs a lesson in humility." He turned to one of the men. "Secure the Baroness and her whore in their tent, and then give these traitors fifty lashes."

"No ...!" Seren cried, futily struggling.

"I beg you ...!" Eloise shouted.

Sir Guldwin smiled wickedly.

"You may ask me again tomorrow, little Baroness. Perhaps, by then, your tongue will have softened enough to persuade me."

"Please ...!" Eloise whined. *"I'll give you anything ...!"*

"Yes, I know," Sir Guldwin said, "You'll give anything ... except the only thing I want: your willing obedience. You offer yourself like a possession I don't already own. In your heart you remain defiant, and that's intolerable; pride in a woman is an unforgivable sin. What are women but fuel for sons, like the firewood we burn to cook our meals? You'll learn what it means to be a woman in my house, little Baroness, and be grateful for the lesson. If your friends don't survive their punishments today, then you'll suffer their lashes tomorrow."

Guards seized her. Kicking and screaming, Eloise and Seren were carried back inside their tent and tied to their chairs, back-to-back, helpless as canaries caged with the cat. Eloise didn't know if Sir Guldwin could still hear her shouted threats, or Seren's colorful curses, or if he'd walked away, supreme in his triumph.

The first crack of the whip struck both women suddenly silent, and they grabbed each other's hands, fearfully holding on. Time passed slowly, and then the lash cracked again.

"Rafe ...!" Seren screamed.

Eloise burst into tears. She didn't know who was getting beaten, Rafe, Karl, or both, but unimaginable torment raged. The man she loved most, and the man who'd become the father she'd never known, were suffering horribly ... because she'd failed.

Eloise and Seren shouted again, promising anything, if they'd only stop. Seren promised every guard acts only prostitutes knew, acts Eloise couldn't believe were possible, yet they ignored her.

Karl and Rafe started to cry out after each blow, and quickly their cries became agonized screams.

Eloise pulled at her bonds until blood flowed upon taut leather knots, thrashing in her chair so hard she almost toppled both of them onto their sides.

Shouting until their voices cracked, Eloise and Seren sat helpless as afternoon dragged on. Night darkened the walls of their tent as they sobbed miserably.

Hysterical, Eloise's mind reeled, struggling to keep a hold on her senses. She'd wanted to be strong like Eric, but she wasn't. Listening to Karl and Rafe scream had seemed an unbearable torment, yet it was nothing compared to the horrible quiet after the floggings stopped. Eloise had called their names, yet only silence answered. Tears poured from her eyes; she didn't know if they were alive or dead. Even in the cave of the Wolflord, she'd never imagined the pain she felt now, worsened by the knowledge that her friends were suffering far worse.

Eloise loved them so much; Rafe had all the qualities she'd dreamed her real father had, emboldened by her mother's stories of his nobility and courage. Rafe was her protector, her friend, and no one's opinion mattered more to her than his. Karl was her lover, and more than that, Eloise loved him. Karl also harbored feelings for Roselyn, yet someday Eloise would be his bride and Karl would be Baron of du Harmonn.

The silence after the last 'crack' was deafening. Neither Karl nor Rafe screamed anymore; *were they still alive?*

Finally, in the middle of the night, Eloise heard muffled voices outside her tent. Eloise steadied herself, and forced back the tears that drenched her cheeks; if Sir Guldwin entered, then she'd surrender to him anything he wanted, even her broken pride, even if she had to kneel down and kiss his boots. Her life was lost; saving her friends was the only good left Eloise could do.

The Seer stuck his head inside her tent and smiled. Shocked, Eloise burst into tears; *they were saved!*

Chapter 2

Hiding in the Swamp

ROSELYN

Pesky insects buzzed about her eyes; the awakening swamp promised a wretched day, and everything reeked of mold. Never had Roselyn awoken so miserably, exhausted and chilled, her feet soaking wet. Roselyn was perched with the others on a small patch of firm ground, nestled amid tall, damp weeds, huddled under the cold, early morning sky. She'd barely slept; they'd been awake most of the night tending the deep lash-wounds on Karl and Rafe. Both were in agony, yet the Seer couldn't drop his illusions to tend them until they were safe, and by then he'd exhausted himself. Several of their cuts needed stitches, but they had no thread or needles.

Roselyn had cringed at her first sight of Karl and Rafe's wounds; she'd seen men beaten before, many times, when some peasant had displeased her father. Yet the depth of these gashes, the swelling of the skin, the long welts and puffy red bruises sickened her. Once she'd dismissed such actions because they were peasants, living the lives God had chosen for them. Now the victims of her father's brutality were the two men she loved most.

Roselyn had been wrong; she'd been taught that peasants were more like animals than the nobility, that they couldn't understand deep thought or grasp emotions outside of their petty, ignoble curse of poverty. Her early upbringing had kept her free of base influences, except for her servants, whom she'd been told were of the best peasant stock. Even as her father's whipped whore, Roselyn had never been sent to a peasant's bed.

A pity she hadn't been sent to Karl's bed: Roselyn would've never left.

Karl: Roselyn still didn't know what to think about him. He confused her, evoked troubled thoughts and unnamed feelings. Karl was born base, a farmer's son. His heart was true, yet his manners were coarse. Was he somewhat simple, or was he honest beyond any Saxon noble? Roselyn loved Karl, despite his dalliance with Eloise, yet she wasn't concerned about their temporary romance; Roselyn wanted Karl forever, and knew he wanted her.

After escaping from her father's army, disguised by the Seer's magic, they'd quickly fled into the lowland swamp. They rode down a narrow deer-trail until the ground became too muddy for the horses, and then they had to dismount and continue on foot.

They'd recovered their most-precious gear. Cloaked in magic, making numerous trips, the Seer had managed to get most of their horses; Karl's stallion was missing, probably killed in the war. He'd located Karl's gambeson, sword, shield, mail and helm, and Eric's shield and helm. Roselyn had her bow and arrows, a sword from one of the guards they'd slain, and she still wore her father's fancy parade armor. The Seer had stolen two canteens. Across his back, the Seer carried his black leather case that bore Eric's severed arm, his heavy sword still tightly-grasped in his dead hand; Roselyn was horrified that he carried the grisly thing.

Sore and wet, Roselyn gingerly pushed back the dew-covered weeds, stretched, and unsuccessfully tried to rub her aching muscles; she couldn't even massage her sore shoulders through the heavy, awkward armor. Slowly she stood, trying not to awaken the others, yet the clanking metal armor sounded like the drunken bar fight she could barely remember.

They were surrounded by still pools of fetid water. They had no food, and they'd emptied their canteens washing out the cuts on Karl and Rafe's backs.

Roselyn hated her father more than ever, yet he was impervious from her contempt. He had their treasure, yet he'd never give up searching for them; once Earl Sir Guldwin laid eyes on anything, land, person, or treasure, he'd never be content until he possessed it entirely.

For the first time in her life, Roselyn had nothing: no family, wealth, or future. The gold and gems of Castle Bristlen were gone, her only hope of purchasing confortable lives for all of them. There'd be no villa in France, no country manor where they could live together in peace. What was her future now? Perhaps she'd become a warrior, as Eric had called her, and fight for a living? Roselyn would've laughed, except she started to cry.

Approaching hoof-beats echoed; Roselyn stood perfectly still, listening. The horse wasn't far away, yet the sound of it grew, then receded as quickly as it'd come; someone had ridden past at great speed. They were still too close to the road, and had to get farther away; once seen, they'd swiftly be recaptured.

With sighs of regret, Roselyn awoke the others. None seemed grateful yet, roused by her tale of hoof-beats, they struggled to their feet.

Their horses still wore their saddles and bridles; the Seer had said to leave them on, in case they needed to flee during the night. Roselyn led her horse quietly down the narrow trail, deeper into the swamp.

Karl fell in line behind her, leading Eric's horse. Karl's face was white, his teeth clenched, yet he uttered no complaint. Rafe was equally silent; Roselyn wished she were as tough as they. She'd never known injuries as severe as theirs, and couldn't imagine taking a single step with the lacerations they bore.

They led their horses, as quietly as possible, farther down the narrow trail, deeper into the swamp. Soon they had to divide their belongings, to unburden their horses as much as possible, to keep them from sinking too deep and breaking a leg. Rafe tried to decline when the Seer gave him Eric's helm and shield, yet everyone insisted. Roselyn gave Rafe her sword, but he was so wounded he used it as a cane.

Their path was torturous, mostly for those behind. The ground was soaked and squished under the slightest weight. Hard hooves sunk deep and shoved most of their trail underwater. Everyone struggled to keep their balance, soaked to their knees. Last in line, the Seer waded through deep water, the skirt of his robe held up, with water-filled boots.

Roselyn didn't regret their journey, although she was so wet she might as well have been swimming. Their footfalls buried the trail behind them, hiding all traces of their passage; not even her father's best hunters could track footprints underwater. Despite its muck and mire, the swamp was their only safe haven.

As the hot sun reached high overhead, thwarted by several disappointing dead ends, the Seer found a large willow tree on rise with mostly-dry dirt underneath. He took Karl's sword, crawled inside, and cut down all of its thin, dead branches, clearing a space so they could stand near its trunk without dried vines hanging in their hair. They tied their horses to a nearby tree, stripped them of saddles and blankets, and crawled inside the waving branches.

Roselyn couldn't sleep. Karl and Rafe quickly passed out on their wet horse blankets, but both moaned, twisting fitfully in their sleep. The Seer sat back against the trunk of the willow and closed his eyes, yet he remained upright, his body stiff. Eloise and Seren quickly followed Rafe and Karl into slumberland.

Unable to sleep with insects buzzing all around, Roselyn sat, her head hung, and wondered what kind of life remained for her; a villain, outcast and hiding, able only to remember having servants, clean clothes, and hearty feasts.

"Roselyn, we're in trouble," the Seer suddenly said, startling her from her reverie. "Your father has a hundred men searching for us, and he's placed bounties of five gold coins on each of our heads."

Roselyn shrugged, not even wondering how the Seer could know this; she'd expected nothing else and feared far worse.

"It may be weeks before we can leave, and we've no food or water."

"I can't go back," Roselyn said. "I defied my father. He'd ...!"

"No worse than he'd do to any of us," the Seer agreed. "How can we survive? We need clean water, lots of it, not only to drink, but to treat Rafe and Karl."

"If we could get back to Madrone ...," Roselyn suggested.

The Seer winced as if struck by a blow.

"We'll find no help there. Sir Guldwin's men broke into my house and ransacked it. My servants are dead, my possessions gone. News of the bounty on our heads has spread throughout the city; every idiot would sell us out. Besides, this isn't the Druid hilltop where Britain's lines of power meet; my arts could never conceal all of us, and our horses, for hours ... or past sentries posted to look for us."

"We can't do anything," Roselyn said. "Rafe might have a better idea. Perhaps we should wake him."

"Let him sleep while he can," the Seer said. "But I'm worried about him and Karl. If their wounds become infected, they'll die."

"Could we go for supplies, just you and I?"

"On foot, it'd take us days. On horseback, we'd likely get caught, and that would mean death for all of us."

"Magic ...?"

"I can't make clean water," the Seer said. "Not out of this muck. Even if we boiled it, I wouldn't trust it, and we can't boil water without a fire, which would bring the hunters right to us. They'll see our smoke in daylight, our flames at night."

"So ... what do we do?"

"Pray."

The others awoke before sunset. Roselyn had tried to sleep but failed. The Seer had gone back into his trance, or fallen asleep, leaning back against the trunk.

Roselyn explained their situation. The others groaned. The presence of so many deep pools of slimy water didn't ease their thirst. Anything was better than sitting, quietly suffering, hungry, miserable, with nothing to do but swat biting insects. Silently Roselyn cursed: *oh, for the sweet days of being chased by thousands of savage Norsemen!*

Roselyn missed Eric. Eric was their real leader, the one who'd saved and kept them together. Without his guidance, where would they be? Sitting helpless in the middle of a swamp? Eric never would've led them here, never tolerated this idleness.

"Thank you!" the Seer said suddenly, coming out of his trance.

"For what?" Roselyn asked.

"For water," the Seer said. "Clean, clear water."

The first spatters were soft, yet soon they began a rapid drumming that rose to a loud drone. Cold drops fell through the branches, awakening every sleeper. Gently the rain fell harder as billowy dark clouds rolled in from the west. The sunlight cut off and drops trickled down the long leaves, soaking them all.

Instead of hiding under them, Rafe had Roselyn, Eloise, and Seren take all of their horse blankets and spread them out over the stumps and bushes. The Seer helped, using his thick black wool cloak, which was woven so finely it held water, and puddles quickly accumulated on them. They filled their canteens as best they could, yet the rain was chill, and soon they were all soaked to the bone; Roselyn's father's armor didn't keep out rain.

Able to stand it no more, Roselyn thumbed the small metal hook that affixed her father's gorget around her neck. Lifting it carefully over her head, she pulled her arms out of its metal vambraces and articulated joints, and then she dropped all of it beside her helm and gauntlets. She slid her thumbs under the silver mail cutting into her shoulders, lifted it up, and tried to pull it off, but it was too heavy; her arms became entwined in the willow branches, and when she tried to jiggle free, she shook the tree and droplets rained upon them.

"Bend over!" Karl and Rafe shouted.

Struggling, Roselyn bent forward as instructed; suddenly her mail slid forward of its own accord, pulled by its weight. However, half of Roselyn's hair seemed caught in the tiny riveted links, and Roselyn fell onto her knees and cried out, her face against the wet ground.

"Hold still ...!" Karl said, and Eloise and Seren gently worked her free.

When the last of her mail fell away, Roselyn cursed like Seren, and reached a hand back to examine her scalp.

"That happens," Karl tried to comfort her.

Roselyn fumed. She was still wearing her father's thick gold trousers, tied around her waist, and his black quilted jacket, both of which were soaked. Her hair was a mess, and she felt chilled and miserable. Roselyn wasn't raised to live like a peasant; she couldn't tolerate weeks of this.

"We have to get out of here ...!" Roselyn hissed, not sure if her words were a request or a demand.

She felt guilty for ordering her friends about like servants, especially since there wasn't anything they could do about it, but the dirty swamp had pushed her limits. She'd hoped she could be strong, but physical suffering was foreign to her. Roselyn hung her head and started to cry.

At dusk, the Seer led Rafe and Karl out into the downpour. Neither had a shirt; the Seer had given each of them a Byzantine silk scarf from his gear, which had strange symbols woven into them, to wear overtop their cuts. Roselyn went with them; she felt guilty for the wounds her father had inflicted.

Rafe knelt first, and rested his weight on his palms. The Seer's cloth was thick with dried blood, yet the Seer insisted they pull it off and let the clean rain wash out their gashes. Slowly Roselyn helped him break the thin cloth from the clinging scabs, and then she washed the fancy cloth out as best she could while the Seer probed Rafe's cuts with deft fingers, cleaning each deeply. When done, they wrung out and replaced the scarf, which clung to his damp skin.

The Seer spoke arcane words of healing, made several mystic gestures, and finally they helped Rafe stand up. Rafe was nearly paralyzed from pain, yet he let them drag him toward their tree, and he slowly staggered back under the willow.

Without hesitation, Karl got down on all fours for the same treatment.

When they finally headed back under the willow, daylight was failing. At Rafe's insistence, since they'd watered the horses and refilled both canteens, Seren helped Rafe gather up their horse blankets and the Seer's cloak. Despite his pains, Rafe carried them under the willow, reached up between the vines, and carefully spread the Seer's cloak over the widest branches. Soon the drops overhead lessened considerably.

"We need some kind of thin rope," Rafe said. "If we could tie our blankets to these branches, then we could make a pavilion, and light a small fire inside it; good wool horse blankets are too thick to let light through."

"Where are you going to find dry wood to build a fire?" Eloise asked.

"One problem at a time," Rafe shrugged. "Unless we find a way to securely tie these blankets to the branches, we can't risk a fire."

"Here," Seren said, and she stood up, drew Roselyn's sword, stabbed the blade through her skirt at the knees, and tore the fabric free. Eloise and Roselyn helped, and they handed the excess cloth to Rafe.

"That'll help," Rafe said.

"I have more," Eloise said.

Standing, Eloise turned her back to the men and fumbled free her laces. She pulled off her outer dress, revealing a thick inner garment, lightly-quilted and soaked with rainwater. Freeing her arms from its shoulder straps, Eloise pulled her overdress back on, then peeled the drenched undergarment down and stepped out of it.

"That'll be plenty," Rafe smiled.

They cut the cloths into long strips, knotted the corners of their blankets, and used the strips to tie them to branches so their edges overlapped. They had to finish the work in total darkness, yet soon they had wet walls around them and a damp roof overhead.

"Now, I'll find dry wood," Rafe said. "Stay here; I'd best do this alone."

Rafe took a sword and went outside. The others stayed under their makeshift shelter, still wearing their soaked clothes, and listened to him thrash through wet bushes. They heard him swing his sword several times, chop wood, and then Rafe pushed inside, trailing the base of a dead tree about three inches thick.

"Give me room," he said in the darkness. "Careful; I've got a drawn sword."

"What're you doing?" the Seer asked.

"I'm carving the wet bark off this branch," Rafe said. "It was fallen but not lying on the ground, so there's dry wood in the middle of it. If someone can think of some way to make a spark ..."

"I have flint," the Seer said.

"Then just be patient," Rafe said. "I've started fires outdoors on Candlemas. If this wood's dry, I'll light it."

Although it seemed to take hours, by feel alone Rafe carved thin, dry slivers out of the center of the branch. Then the Seer carefully passed him the tiny piece of flint he carried, and Rafe scraped it against the inside of Roselyn's steel vambrace. Sudden flashes of sparks seemed blinding, and soon Rafe had a single spark glowing on a thin, dry wood shaving, and he masterfully fed it and kept it alive until it flamed. Rafe carved more shavings, which Karl fed to their tiny flame. Soon they piled larger pieces upon it, and set the wet bark nearby it to dry.

Light revealed a miserable group, drenched and shivering. Eloise and Seren were holding each other for warmth and the Seer's teeth were chattering.

"Do we need more wood?" Eloise asked.

"Not yet," Rafe said, carving off bigger pieces of wet bark. "Once it gets warm in here then we'll only want to keep a small fire going, preferably just coals; we don't want bright light. There are watchers on the hilltops in every direction, despite the rain, just waiting for us to give away our position."

"We're never going to get warm in wet clothes," the Seer said.

"I was waiting until it got warm to say that," Rafe said.

Fifteen minutes later, when the smoky air was considerably warmer, Rafe stood up.

"Well, the longer we wait, the sicker we'll get," he said. "Ladies, if you want to look away, do so now."

Roselyn shielded her eyes with her hand, not waiting to see if Eloise and Seren did the same. She heard Rafe peel off his wet clothes and forced herself not to look: Rafe was wearing nothing but his boots, trousers, and the silk bandage on his back. Then she heard him squat back down.

"My turn," said the Seer's voice, and Roselyn squeezed her eyelids tightly.

"Hey, you're half-dry!" Karl complained.

"Correction: I'm half-drowned," the Seer said. "You should've bought more appropriate travel-clothes."

"Hang your stuff on a branch," Rafe said. "Don't spread it out. Leave the women some room."

Roselyn shivered; it'd taken Eric and Karl's lives to get her to ride naked into the midst of Svenson's killers, pretending to be a Valkyrie. The idea of sitting here all night, men and women, all unclothed, was unthinkable. Her strict upbringing, and church teachings, rebelled at the very idea of it, and her mother would've died at its mere suggestion.

"Me turn," Seren said.

Roselyn clenched her jaw. She was wet, freezing, and had no choice.

Chapter 3

Hope

KARL

The sun rose with infinite slowness. Karl leaned back on one elbow, propped against a saddle, the lashes on his back preventing him from sleeping. Their fire was a small pile of dying embers; it had to go out before dawn, when Sir Guldwin's sentries would spot the smoke. Karl had volunteered to watch the fire, to keep it going all night, as he'd often done at home during the snows. Karl figured he might as well, since he wasn't going to get any rest with Roselyn and Eloise sleeping naked only an arm's reach away.

He tried not to look, yet failed more often than not; several times he built up the fire for light, then let it burn down when guilt overwhelmed desire. Eloise and Roselyn liked to be respected, like they were men; Karl wasn't going to earn respect by staring at their naked breasts while they slept. Karl felt justified, since they'd both slept with him, yet he was also worried, remembering their revenge under the willows of the Druid hilltop. Did they really expect him to choose between them, to decide which of their affections he preferred? How could he do that when he obviously loved them both?

Karl foundered. He loved Roselyn the most, he knew, yet Eloise was so delicious, so demanding, that Karl had no idea what to do. He wanted them both, yet they were noblewomen, and wouldn't stand his indecision for long. Worse, by doing nothing, he might insult them both, and they'd leave him forever.

Karl ground his teeth in frustration. It was too warm inside their shelter; several times he'd pulled aside their hanging blankets to let in cool air and disperse the smoke. Unlike their still-wet boots, their hanging clothes were mostly dry; he'd checked them several times during the night, and shifted them on their branches whenever they needed it. But what good was that? When everyone woke up, their clothes would be dry enough, but where would they go? Earl Sir Guldwin's troops wouldn't give up their search because it'd rained.

Rafe and the Seer slept quietly, curled close but not touching. Eloise and Roselyn slept cuddled, but Seren had a fitful sleep; she twitched, her hands shook, and twice bolted upright as if from some frightful dream. Karl tried to calm her without staring at her, yet more than once his eyes strayed to her while she slept. Seren wasn't as firm or slender as Roselyn or Eloise, yet she had large, round breasts, thick nipples, and the skin below her shoulders bore few of the tiny wrinkles that crossed her face and neck. Whenever she awoke, Karl whispered softly to Seren, and tried to soothe the fears that had startled her from her sleep. Eventually Seren thanked him and curled up against Eloise and Roselyn to go back to sleep.

Shortly after dawn, Rafe yawned loudly enough to wake the others. Their fire extinguished, Karl dressed in his tunic and went outside to give them more room ... and avoid the temptation to stare at the women while they were awake.

Outside, Karl tried not to brush his dry clothes against wet leaves, but they surrounded him. Karl was barefoot, his wet boots piled with the shoes of the others inside their shelter, and the ground was damp and cold. His stomach growled: Karl couldn't remember when he'd last eaten, yet he couldn't wait much longer. Soon they'd have to go somewhere with food ... no matter how dangerous traveling was.

Karl picked up a fallen switch and flicked it at all the nearby leaves, knocking off what thick droplets he could. Perhaps, when the others emerged, they wouldn't get their dry clothes wet again.

Eloise emerged from their shelter first, her dry red dress clinging only slightly less than when it was drenched, revealing much more of her thin shape without her bulky undergarments. Karl smiled, watching her comb tangles out of her hair with her fingers. Then Eloise glanced up at Karl, and frowned as if she knew he'd been staring at her nakedness; Karl blushed deeply.

Seren stumbled out of their tent looking haggard, aged, as if she hadn't slept at all. Karl wished her a good morning, but she scowled at him and angrily scratched and picked at her arms, so he shut up and let her be.

The others came out slowly, one by one. The rain had stopped, yet every leaf and blade of grass sported thick beads of sparkling dew. The trees were dripping, ready to deluge upon anyone that shook them. The early sunlight was warm, causing a thin, wafting mist to rise off of the still ponds. Noisy insects and frogs surrounded them, as did annoying gnats and the occasional buzzing dragonfly.

Rafe picked up another fallen branch and began repeating Karl's attack, knocking off more drops.

"Where to today?" Karl asked as the Seer emerged.

"To ...?" the Seer frowned. "We can't leave. Today we try and find whatever food's here."

"Here ...? Here's nowhere!"

"Nowhere's our only hope," the Seer said. "Hundreds are searching for us. If we leave this swamp then we'll be captured ... and worse."

"There must be a way ..."

"There isn't," the Seer said. "This is our home ... until the searchers go away."

"What if they come here? Maybe we should keep moving ...?"

"They're searching for us north of here. They won't come this far south, and we mustn't go far from camp or draw them to us. I'm the leader; we stay here until its safe."

"Who made you leader ...?" Karl argued.

"You promised to follow me if I saved you from Svenson's wizard," the Seer insisted. "I've saved you twice now: without me, you'd be getting your morning lashes from Earl Sir Guldwin, and I alone can help keep evil vapors out of your wounds. I've more than kept my half of our bargain, and now it's time you proved your worth. We stay here, for weeks, if necessary, and then follow Eric."

"Follow Eric ...?" Karl asked. "You ... you want us to ... *die?"*

"Can't you understand anything?" the Seer sneered. "Those yellow marks I made on Eric's boots, remember? The glowing prints ...? They were more powerful than even my Masters knew. We used them to track our own, but only while they were alive. I never imagined that they'd work past life."

"But ... *Eric's dead!"*

"Dead, yes, but not lost. Every step his spirit takes, while it walks in shadow, marks its path, leaving a trail. I saw his prints on the battlefield, yellow 'V's glowing in the light of my moonstone, leading away from his fallen corpse."

"You're insane," Karl whispered, his lips stretching diagonally.

"I told you, before we left Madrone, about all of us following Eric's tracks through an old forest at night. I never guessed Eric would be dead, his ghost making the tracks, but that doesn't matter; we must follow Her plan as She has shown it to me, and learn the rest as we go."

"Go where ...?"

"You'll know as soon as I do."

"You're mad!" Karl exclaimed. "Utterly mad!"

The Seer stepped forward angrily. Karl stiffened, rose up to his full height, and towered over the small, black-robed Druid.

"Enough ...!" Rafe shouted, and he pushed between them, although the pain bent him over and made him gasp. "Listen to yourselves! Seer: you're babbling nonsense. However, you're right: we promised to follow you, and we can't leave here without getting caught."

"No ...!" Seren hissed suddenly, frightfully shrill. *"We have to ... get out! Now! This place filthy, with ... things ... crawling ...!"*

Suddenly Seren screamed, staring at her arms as if they were poisonous. She trembled, shrieked, and jumped up and down, flailing frantically.

"Get them off ...!" Seren screamed. *"Get them off me ...!"*

"Seren ...!" Rafe shouted as she collapsed and fell to the ground, thrashing wildly among wet leaves, foaming at the mouth. Rafe jumped to help her, the Seer beside him.

"What is it ...?" the Seer cried. *"A spell ...?"*

"No, she's Bug-Picking!" Rafe said. "She's got The Shakes, like some people get when they haven't had a drink for a while."

"Where're the canteens?" Roselyn asked.

"Canteens won't help," Rafe said, easily pinning her arms with his strong hands. "She needs whiskey or beer, and we don't have any. We've got to hold her still until this passes: hold her legs and head. She could hurt herself, shaking this badly."

"She'll get us killed!" the Seer seethed. *"Cover her mouth! Don't let her scream!"*

While Seren thrashed, Eloise and Roselyn each tried to hold still one of her legs. Seren kicked and struggled, fighting them all. Seren was surprisingly limber, although little strength backed her blows. Karl held her head and kept one hand pressed firmly over her screaming mouth, muffling her shouts so Earl Sir Guldwin's searchers wouldn't hear.

Seren was no match for their combined strength. Eventually she faded into an exhausted, fitful sleep. The men lifted and carried Seren back inside their shelter, letting her sleep where it was warm. Roselyn and Eloise stayed with her.

At the Seer's suggestion, Karl and Rafe went hunting and foraging, yet they found only four tiny bird's eggs and some early blueberries. Dismayed, the Seer used his magic and called forth a big rabbit, which hopped right into his lap ... before Karl grabbed it and twisted its neck.

Time passed agonizingly slow. Seren had several more seizures over the next few days, but none as serious as the first. The Seer gave her a tiny vial containing some wine that he called a component, but it was too little to help. Yet she slowly improved, and afterwards thanked everyone for helping her.

Several others felt ill, although not as bad as Seren. Alcohol was so commonly drunk, at every meal, none but Rafe was surprised when they began suffering its lack.

Karl and Rafe's wounds healed nicely; the Seer washed and chanted daily healing spells over them, yet they appreciated his help silently.

Over two weeks passed, each day as miserable as the last. Mosquitoes ate them alive, when it wasn't raining, which it seemed to do every day, which let them collect clean water as it streamed off of their makeshift tent. They stayed inside their shelter when they could, spoke little, and gathered firewood or hunted, which became easier after Karl carved twin-pronged spears for hunting frogs and lizards.

Some evenings, one or another of them would try to lift everyone's spirits by telling a story or singing a song, yet it did little good. The only thing that eased their pain was talking about Eric.

The moon waxed, almost full, before the Seer announced that the searchers had finally left. Little cheer greeted this news; although relieved, no enthusiasm remained. They crawled out of the swamp filthy, sore, and more miserable than ever.

The Seer led them back to the battlefield where Eric and Svenson had both fallen, fighting to their mutual deaths. Save for countless broken arrows, the stench of blood, and scraps of cloth, the only remaining sign of the battle was a large mound of charred bodies, thousands of Vikings, stacked, covered with wood, and set to torch. The men briefly investigated it, braving its huge swarm of flies. The women refused to approach the sickening mound.

"Follow me," the Seer said, and he took out his moonstone and spurred, slowly riding north across the battlefield.

They rode after him for about half an hour, across and away from the battlefield, on a trail leading back to the main road, and then the Seer halted and raised his enchanted moonstone high.

"There ...!" he cried to all of them, pointing.

On the ground, under the thick branches of a wide tree, clearly visible, was a dim glowing 'V', its tip pointing north like an arrowhead aimed at the unknown.

"Well, Karl ...?" the Seer asked. "On your honor, is that not the mark I scribed on Eric's boots?"

Karl growled in annoyance, slowly dismounted, and approached the glowing 'V'. It wavered weakly in the gray morning light. He knelt to examine it, reached out a finger and touched it; it instantly vanished.

"It's gone!" Karl said.

"Any disturbance destroys it, even heavy rain, so they'll be hard to find," the Seer said. "But they are what I said: tracks made by Eric's ghost ... as he walks unseen."

"That's impossible," Karl said, although no conviction backed his words.

"Where else do you have to go ...?" the Seer asked. "We're outlaws with prices on our heads. We can't stay here. I can get us real food and drink, if this trail leads where I think it will."

"I'll go ... for now," Rafe moaned. "If the devil himself offered me some baked chicken and beer, at this moment, I'd accept."

Reluctant agreement murmured. None seemed excited, yet the prospect of real food after weeks of reptiles and tiny amphibians was more than they could refuse. The Seer rode ahead, holding his moonstone before him, and the others trailed behind.

Karl scowled, disgusted; the Seer was insane, carrying his grisly back leather case strapped across his back with Eric's bloody sword and arm tightly sealed inside of it. Yet Karl followed, not just because Roselyn and Eloise followed, but also because the Seer had spoken the truth: Karl had nowhere else to go.

The warm sun rose into the sky. It felt good to be traveling again. After weeks of confinement in the swamp, cramped and cold with nothing to do, having a horse beneath him and miles of warm, dry fields seemed like Heaven. If only Eric had been riding beside them, his burlap bag bulging with stolen gold, his knavish mind devising deceptive plots, then it would've been paradise. But Eric was gone, dead on the battlefield, and they'd finished their mourning. Eric's absence was met with mixed feelings among the companions; they all missed his confident smile and deep belly-laughs, but at least they didn't have to worry about becoming entangled in any more wild, dangerous adventures.

The fire on Karl's back had finally cooled, enough that Karl could wear his gambeson and mail again. It'd been a painful two weeks, yet the Seer's healing spells had done wonders. Karl and Rafe had heavy scars, which the Seer said would never fade, but their pain was gone, and comfort was all Karl cared about.

He hated Sir Guldwin; each time that lash had struck, until he passed out, all Karl wanted was a lash of his own, with Guldwin hanging between two posts. Yet the pain was so much more intense than he'd ever imagined; Karl wasn't sure if he could lash anyone like that. If Karl ever wanted to kill a man, then he'd do it quickly; no one deserved torture.

Eloise and Roselyn had never left their camp in the swamp. Without privacy, Karl hadn't once gotten the chance to confront them. They'd politely declined his every attempt to get either of them alone, as if playing another mischievous game. Yet Karl was determined to end their game soon; eventually one of them would have to talk to him.

Crossing empty grazelands under the first blue sky he'd seen in a week, Karl relaxed and enjoyed the clean air. The Seer planned for them to rest early, and begin again after dark, so they could ride through populated lands unseen. A bounty still hung on their heads; they couldn't afford rumors of them to reach Guldwin's searchers.

The glowing 'V's unnerved Karl. They found very few, and many times the Seer would scout ahead or just guess at which direction they should be heading. He insisted that rains had destroyed most of the marks, and that otherwise they'd be as easy to trace as deer tracks across a muddy field.

No one believed the marks were ghostly footprints left by Eric's spirit; Karl suggested that the Seer might be creating them as he rode ahead, probably leading them into some trap. Yet Rafe said it didn't matter which direction they took; he was glad just to leave Earl Sir Guldwin's lands, and the Seer was their best hope of escape. Once they climbed the foothills back into du Harmonn, then they'd be in Eloise's lands, as safe as they could be until they got away from England.

Roselyn's idea of sailing to France seemed appealing, and still stood as their eventual destination, although they had no means to purchase transportation across the sea.

"Stop ...!" cried a deep, angry voice from nowhere. "Athelwynne, stop ...!"

As if an invisible veil was pulled away, suddenly a line of people stood blocking their path. They were plain Saxons wearing simple, old clothes, looking rather tired and sad, yet their sudden manifestation belied unknown menace. Karl drew his sword, yet stayed mounted.

One stranger, a tall, white-bearded man dressed in thick gray robes, stood slightly ahead of the others.

"Athelwynne, halt ...!" he cried.

The Seer reined in, seeming not at all surprised.

"Master ...!" the Seer grinned, looking down upon the old man from his horse. "What're you doing here? They didn't kick you off the Hidden Island, too, did they?"

"You were never kicked off, Athelwynne," the Master said gruffly. "You had to be sent away for your own good. You never would've left willingly."

"Why ...?" the Seer demanded, an angry sneer deepening his voice. "So I could give up the most important studies of my life for the chance to freeze in the wild, and then starve in the streets, reading palms for food?"

"We loved you ..."

"You feared me."

"We feared what you might become," the Master said. "It isn't good for one student to excel so much. It denies humility and invites ambition."

"Loss of dominance, you mean," the Seer scoffed. "What do you want?"

"I want nothing," the Master said. "We've come to save you from your mad quest."

"I'm serving the Lady," the Seer said. "She sent visions to me, directly, and I'm doing Her bidding."

This announcement startled the strangers, and each glanced worriedly at the others. Even the Master seemed shaken, yet he didn't back down.

"Visions from the Lady should've been reported to the Druid High Council at once!" the Master said.

"If the Lady wished for the Council to know then She'd have told you," the Seer said. "The Council doesn't speak for all Druids. You abandoned me; how dare you ask for support ...?"

"Pride is your weakness," the Master said. "It'll kill you someday, Athelwynne."

"Why should I give up my quest?" the Seer demanded. "For your sake?"

"I'd think that those who trained you could ask anything of you, but that would require gratitude," the

Master said. "We're here on behalf of Fairie, who asked us to intercede."

"My quest has no bearing on Fairie," the Seer said.

"Much of Fairie lore isn't told to mortals," the Master said. "The doorway you seek is their only escape from this world; it mustn't be found."

"I won't abandon my duty," the Seer said. "If the innocents of Fairie would convince me, then they must do so with reasons."

"Then we'll have to meet with them," the Master said. "They're not far."

"Really ...?" the Seer asked. "I never knew there was a Sacred Well near Madrone."

"As always, fairies prefer to live in secret," the Master said. "Your companions can wait here."

"My companions are people of honor, more than exists on this Council," the Seer said. "I'm in a hurry, but I'll follow, if it means my companions may experience Fairie. It'd do them good, I think, and prove my value as leader. Take us, Master, or stand aside; you don't wish to battle me."

"Your spirit has grown dark," the Master sneered. "I pray the inhabitants of Fairie may shed some illumination upon it before it turns completely black."

The Master turned to an older woman standing quietly behind him. They spoke no words, yet exchanged meaningful glances. She looked up at the Seer, shook her head sadly, and then turned away. As she walked, all of the other Druids turn to follow her ... at a respectful distance.

"Dismount and lead your horses on foot," the Seer whispered. "We'll leave them outside of our destination ... with all of our weapons ... and any hurtful thoughts. Don't do anything hasty! We're entering a world older than ours."

"Why ...?" Karl asked. "They've no horses. We could just ride around ..."

"Don't be an ass!" the Seer snapped. "How far do you think we'll get with the entire Druid Council against us?"

Karl glared, yet he sheathed his sword. He didn't like the Seer or his magic; the last thing he wanted was more Druids. Already he felt like an idiot, growing up believing that all faiths were deceptions, all believers fools. Now he'd seen fantastic illusions and Valkyrie; Karl didn't need any more proof of what a fool he was.

In silence, the old woman led them miles across empty hills and seldom-used trails. Around noon, they walked down to the edge of another wetland marsh surrounded by fir trees and small stagnant pools. Rafe quickly gathered the bridles of all their horses and tied them together, so the horses stood in a circle, facing each other. Then the Seer spread out his cloak upon the grass and placed his small silver knife upon it. At his direction, all disarmed themselves, leaving even shields and helms. Then the Druid woman led them into the mire, down a thin, dry trail barely visible between thick bushes.

Their path led to a wide, grassy, circular clearing, roofed by long, leafy branches. No signs existed that they were in a marsh; Karl was reminded of the Druid hilltop more than the swamp they'd hidden in. The air smelled sweet, filled with birdsong, and bright flowers sprouting colorful blossoms gleamed everywhere. Warmth filled the clearing, as if its thick roof of leaves was letting in sunlight unscathed by shadows, and a calm, delighted contentment washed over him; never before had Karl been there, yet he had the unmistakable feeling he'd come home.

In the center of the clearing, a wide ring of white stones outlined a still, clear well, brimming with water, sparkling in the sunlight. At the water's edge, the old woman knelt on the white stone ring, bowed, and kissed the water's smooth surface. Ringlets flowed outwards where her lips disturbed its still water, and underneath the water, an elfin face smiled back.

"They've come, as I promised," the old woman said to the face in the well.

The elvin face nodded, and then water burst upwards; four small guards, waist-tall men wearing fish-scale armor, splashed up from the pool, brandishing spears of polished bone. Surrounding the well protectively, the four guards dipped their spears back into the water and raised from the pool a tiny elfin woman of exquisite beauty, clad in rainbow veils like dragonfly wings bound by golden ribbons. Each of her hands laid lightly upon two of their crossed speartips, and she rose to stand upon the well's surface as if she weighed less than a feather.

Smiling, she stood mere inches taller than her guards, and upon her head shone a crown of tiny stars that brightened the clearing with a soft, radiant glow.

She released the spears, stood unsinking upon the water, and leaned forward to kiss the old woman. Then the old man came forward and knelt, and she bowed to him.

Laughing voices erupted from the eerie silence. Tiny folk came out, dancing into the clearing from behind every bush and tree. Closed flower buds opened to sprout more tiny fairies. Hundreds of wee folk emerged, some knee high, a few taller, but most tiny enough to curl up in your palm, and some only points of brilliant light dancing on translucent wings.

The Seer knelt, as did all the Druids, and the companions followed their lead.

Awestruck, Karl gaped before inhuman beauty. The fairies looked like creatures from impossible dreams, beautiful without blemish, tiny, yet more spectacular than any illusion of man or giant. They cavorted freely, with infinite grace and comic abandon, such that they emanated pure joy to those watching, and their sheer numbers seemed impossible, as if there were always more every time he looked. Many fairies seemed to be intently observing the companions, cautious or delighted, while others appeared blissfully unaware of their presence.

"Welcome," said the elfin lady, her voice tinkling like glass bells ringing in the wind as she stepped from the well onto grass. "I am Titania, First Princess of Fairie, Governess of all Fairie on the Western Isles. Please, friends, sit and be calmed. We mean no harm to any son of man. We only seek to protect ourselves from man's violent nature."

"We seek harm to none who let us pass in peace," the Seer said abruptly, his voice harsh and grating compared to hers. "Most beautiful Titania, never would we willingly allow harm to you or yours; I swear my life upon this."

"We know your word is true," Titania smiled. "We're aware of your quest, and glad are our hearts to see loyalty among humans to a fallen friend. We rejoice in any sign that someday peace may reign between our sundered races. Yet, for centuries, we've seen all signs of hope greatly outnumbered by tragedies of human cruelty. Beside yours, our folk are frail as morning mists that scatter and fade. We're scattered now, and all portents warn of our fade, yet I'll delay that day as long as I can, while this beautiful land remains open to us."

"May it ever remain open," the Seer bowed.

"And though the sun must rise," the Master said, "should someday it set, may this world be yours again."

Titania bowed silently, her very movement musical, flowing with quiet grace.

"I thank you all," Titania said. "Yet I dare not forget my duty to Fairie. Your quest, which I praise, gravely endangers my folk. The passage you seek, the 'crack in the world', lies hidden at the edge of your mortal reality, and is meant only for those who never return. Would you, for love of your lost friend, venture forever from this world of sun and moon?"

"Not I, unless the Lady commands it," the Seer said, and her bright gaze passed from him to Karl.

"Nor I," Karl quickly said, without thinking, and her sweet eyes went on to stare at each of them in turn. Roselyn, Rafe, and Eloise answered quickly. Then her eyes fell on Seren.

"You enchant me, Mother Fairie, all choice taken?" Seren asked.

"No, sweet child," Titania smiled. "I ask your heart, which is true beyond words."

"Wish no harm to little folk. Revere in heart, like when young. Blessed be, Great Mother." Seren bowed deeply.

"Blessed be, sweet child," Titania smiled. "Blessed be all, yet I can't condone this quest by words spoken in peace. To give you leave, I'd have to put one of you to a fearsome test, which I fain wouldn't, for it's dangerous beyond the strengths of men; few have ever survived. Abandon thy quest, depart in peace, and live long."

"No," the Seer said. "If there's a way, then show me the path. Only I can lead these folk on the Lady's road, so if our journey ends now, let it be upon my head."

"Or mine," Roselyn said quickly. "I ... loved Eric."

Slowly Karl dragged his eyes away from Titania's enchantment and gazed at Roselyn.

Roselyn loved Eric ...?

Was she mad, or ensorcelled? Surely she didn't believe the Seer's tale, that Eric was a wandering ghost leaving glowing footprints.

"I'll suffer your test," Eloise said slowly, "if only to spare my companions. I need them ... and love them."

Karl stared at Eloise.

They're both mad, Karl thought.

"No, I go," Seren said, taking Rafe's hand in hers. "Me life be small loss."

"Nay, I'll take this test," Rafe said. "I slew the Wolflord, and I'll do so again, if need be."

Incredulously Karl stared at his companions.

Were they all insane?

Finally he looked at Titania, noticing all eyes watching him.

"Yea, I'll go," Karl said with a heavy sigh. "If one of us must, it should be me; I fight the best."

"Very well," Titania said softly. "Close your eyes, all of you. I'll choose one, and they must go. Your test shall be to slay a great enemy of ours, a monster in the well. There are many, yet only one need be slain to achieve my test. Beware, for they are violent warriors who delight only in combat. Should another come before you have slain one, it won't bode well for you. But each creature slain is a victory for Fairie, so fight hard, if you'd prove yourself and your companions. In this shall we learn the value of your oaths."

A sudden gust blew through the clearing, and Karl seemed at once tired and dizzy. He closed his eyes to a swirl of vertigo and reached out to keep from falling, yet his hand felt nothing, no rock, tree, ground, or grass. Then Titania's pure, sweet voice splashed upon him like fresh, clean water.

"As you said, dear Karl, you are best suited for this challenge. Arise, take your sword, walk to the edge of the well, and take a deep breath. To enter the world of the creatures, leap blindly into our well. Open your eyes underwater, and you'll see their lair. May you find only one! They'll instantly smell your blood and approach. Strike hard and fast, Karl, for the air they breathe is the foulest poison to men and Fairie alike, and you must slay one and return through the well in the space of a single breath."

Oh, great, Karl thought. *Why always him?* Yet he couldn't back down. He wanted to: backing down would put an end to this 'Eric's ghost' nonsense, and maybe they could drop the Seer into the well and leave him behind, too. Yet that would make Karl look like a coward before Titania, and she was so beautiful, so magical, Karl wasn't sure if he could bear it. Roselyn and Eloise certainly wouldn't be impressed if he backed out now, and that decided the matter.

Karl opened his eyes, yet everything was foggy, distorted, as if he were suddenly dreaming. Two of the taller fairies stood before him, holding out his shining sword, gleaming in the sunlight. He took his sword, inhaled a deep breath, and stepped toward the well.

This test was insane!

Why hadn't the Valkyrie just taken Eric, instead of charging him with the task? Karl had no quarrel with monsters of Fairie that breathed poison! But, so what? Since he'd met Eric, everything he'd done was crazy.

Karl inhaled again, drew his deepest breath, closed his eyes, and leaped into the water.

Nerves screamed against the cold wet, yet, withstanding the shock, he kept his wits, breath, and let the weight of his mail carry him down until his boots struck mud. Then he opened his eyes; a wide tunnel yawned, streaming with waving rays of diffused light.

Karl swam quickly; movement was easy; the walls were so close Karl merely pulled himself along and up. Yet, as he neared the surface, Karl saw not sunlight, but firelight's red flicker. Karl broke the surface in a large cave swirling with thick, menacing brown mists. He dared not breathe, remembering Titania's warning, and splashed out of the small circular pool. The cavern was empty, save for a driftwood fire and the deadly, ever-churning brown mists.

His lungs began to cramp. Karl held his free hand over his mouth and nose to keep from breathing the poison.

Where was it ...?

Titania had said the monsters would come instantly! Yet he stood alone in the light of the small fire.

Eyes bulged, chest constricting. A moment more Karl hesitated, yet nothing came, and Karl could wait no longer. He bent to jump in, to swim back before his breath failed.

Abruptly the mist-swept pool splashed upwards. Out climbed a mass of matted seaweed, towering over him. Dying to breathe, Karl lunged forward and stabbed through the heart of the monstrous hulking mass.

It didn't fall; it charged. Karl sidestepped and slashed hard, repeatedly, yet his sword-strikes showed no effect.

Another splash, like a knock on Hell's door, made Karl turn. Another creature had come. With all his strength, Karl swung his razor-edged blade down to crush the creature's skull. Karl struck, hard and true, yet the creature remained unhurt, as if Karl were a mere annoyance.

Suddenly its arms wrapped about Karl's waist, as if it were wrestling. Karl toppled, the monster with him. It dropped atop of him, and they slammed against hard rock. Karl's lungs burst, and instinctively he gasped, feeling burning brown mists rake down his throat.

Poison ...!

Karl was dead, with nothing left but to wonder how long it would take, and whether or not it would hurt. It'd been a strange life, a stranger way to die. Yet he broke free of the monster's grasp; if Karl was doomed, then he'd die with more honor than he'd shown fleeing Castle Bristlen.

The fight was impossible. No matter how hard Karl struck, his sword wouldn't even dent the heavy shells these monsters wore underneath their layers of seaweed. Another monster pulled itself from the pool; four monsters filled the cave, hacking and clawing at each other with sudden fury, when slowly Karl's eyes began to darken, his head to throb.

The poison was taking effect ...!

Karl fell, too weak to stand. His burning throat closed, his ears heard no longer. The creature he'd been fighting turned suddenly and ran to the pool, yet another beast intercepted it, and they began fighting.

Karl couldn't even care any longer. He'd done his best. He closed his eyes to die.

Karl could almost hear the growls and screams of the monsters turn to grunts of his companions, and the stomps of booted feet upon grass. Then he distinctly heard Rafe's wheezing cough.

Karl was shivering, drenched, yet awake and alive, fallen upon the gentle grass of the Fairie clearing, hearing the tinkling laughter of the tiny folk.

Or was he dead ...?

Karl raised his sword, fearing some evil vision, yet found he clutched only a bruised willow branch.

Rafe knelt before him, another willow branch in his hand, raised to strike Eloise, who was holding her branch to block his, as were Seren and Roselyn, facing each other with willow branches by the well, all blinking stupidly. All stood, as soaking wet as Karl, hair draggled, clothes clung tight.

Mocking laughter erupted from the Seer, who sat at ease beside Titania, echoed by thousands of tiny folk, giggling while they danced.

"Peace!" Titania cried. "Let all fighting cease! There are no monsters, no poisons, no danger. The test is over. You've proven your words, for even after you each thought yourselves to have breathed fatal poison, all remained, fighting what you thought were our enemies. We can ask no more of you. You're free to take any path you desire ... with the blessings of Fairie."

"Well done!" the Seer laughed. "Most entertaining!"

"Sarcasm ill becomes your station, Athelwynne," the Master sneered. "As my pupil, never did you scorn others, or find mirth in discomfort; once you were a Druid, but you've changed."

"Changed to survive the real world," the Seer scowled. "Sacred holies become rare after being cast out: cruelly I learned this."

"Then you learned nothing," the Master said. "The Lady sees Her people always, and nothing happens to them but by Her will. All we can do is choose the courses She puts before us, rather than our own. As it is said: Wisdom is a mountaintop; the road is always uphill, and while other paths may be easier, the view shall never be as great."

"I ...? Choose the easy path ...?" the Seer asked. "To the edge of this world ... and through a deadly doorway to the next? What greater challenge would you have me face?"

"The path inward," the Master said, furrowing his thick brows. "Here you stand, a Druid priest, leading Christian Saxons on a quest to the lair of the Norse Gods. Is this the path the Lady sets for you, or do you not seek beyond yourself? Have you no humility, nor courage to accept earthly limits? For whose sake dare you take up this quest? Our Lady's ...? Your dead Viking's ...?"

"For power," the Seer said arrogantly. "Think you I gave up Her when She gave up me? Long I followed Her teachings, preaching, presiding over Beltane and Candlemas, and starving in the streets, ignored by our people, scorned and mocked by Christians. Why? Because they have power! Their own faiths they've plundered, purging true paths for coined profits. Why would they seek wisdom in the Lady's name when they reject the writings of their own dead God?"

"As your teacher and I," the old woman said, "many Christians devoutly follow their own faith, misled though some may be by a few vain priests. Druids have suffered similar difficulties. As for those Christians who turn aside from their teachings, will you scorn them, so like yourself?"

The Seer looked away.

"I love the Lady, but I can't lead Her way where She isn't. I won't be a Christian priest, raining guilt, twisting intentions, and choking choices. This quest will grant me the power to prove Her glory still lives."

"Who sees not Her power?" Titania laughed. "She rises each morning and watches over us each night. She grows life for our food, homes, and colors the world from each blowing leaf to every grain of sand. Who opens their eyes and sees not Her splendor?"

"Blessed are fairies, whose eyes see," the Seer smiled. "Perhaps that's the doom of men, that we live blind amid the Lady's splendor."

"Fairie eyes see the same as human eyes, yet never grow so weary of the sights that they forget to look," the Master said.

"The day is passing," Titania said to the Seer. "Your friends are free to go, but you, who proved resistant to our glamour, must now earn the trust of Fairie."

"And how, great princess, may I do that?" the Seer asked.

"We'd trust you, Druid priest, were this quest not so perilous. Since we can't test you as the others, you must give us your oath," Titania said. "Swear now, before all of my people, that you shall cast your body and soul into molten fire before you see harm come to the talisman I now give you, save only to keep it from falling into evil hands, and should you return again to this world, you will seek out this well and into it return this charm."

Titania stretched out her hand, holding before the Seer an egg of glowing white crystal hanging from a loop of leafy vine.

"My lady ...!" the Seer cried. "A gift of Fairie ...! I'm honored beyond words! Hear now my pledge: this gift I will guard with my very life and soul, upon threat of molten fire, and no harm shall come to it while breath stirs within me, and should ever I return to this world, my first quest shall be to return here, as you command, to cast your talisman into this well."

"And we of Fairie do hear your words and make of ourselves this pledge," Titania said. "Great reward shall we bestow after the manner of our kind, honor with trust, diligence with praise, oathbreaking with vengeance. So say I, Titania, Queen of the Western Isles. But again, I warn you, for this can't be forgotten: you mustn't allow this talisman to fall into evil hands, even if you must destroy it."

"I so swear," the Seer promised.

"Then I no longer restrain you," Titania said. "Go now. The moon waxes late tonight, and you must ride far 'ere it rises. Take our blessings, yet watch your footsteps, even in darkness, and may the Lady light your way."

The Seer bowed before heading back down the thin trail, to where their horses and weapons lay. Seren walked forward towards Titania, shyly bowed, and then turned to follow. Rafe repeated Seren's example, and Roselyn and Eloise followed his. Karl followed Eric's example: Karl walked forward, sloshing in his wet clothes and armor, and picked up Titania as he would his youngest sister.

"Blessed be, Titania the Beautiful, and if my word has any worth at all, then blessings upon you and all your happy folk!"

Karl kissed Titania's white forehead, and then set her down gently, ignoring the threatening spears of her annoyed guardsmen.

"Great worth have your blessings," Titania smiled up at Karl. "Bold as you are, perhaps your bravery will save us all."

"Where did you get that?" Eloise asked as they emerged from the marsh.

Karl looked down; tucked into his belt was one of Titania 's golden ribbons, shimmering with many colors.

"I don't know," Karl smiled.

Eloise glared at Karl as they gathered their belongings and rode back the way they'd come. A wind, unusually warm, blew strongly across the fields, and Karl was unsurprised to find their wet clothes, even his quilted gambeson and leather boots, bone-dry before they reached the road.

Chapter 4

Easy Rambling

SEREN

All the lands away from Madrone were totally new to Seren. When young, she'd often climbed onto the smoky rooftops of Madrone, and from their heights viewed the only horizons she'd ever known. Seren had never walked more than an hour from her city's familiar bustle, and the brothel in which she'd been born. She'd feared to wander too far, yet now she felt utterly safe. Rafe and his friends were stronger than she'd guessed, and had conquered foes more terrible than she'd ever imagined. They were like a wild, fresh wind in her aged gray hair, and in their company Seren felt protected.

The Seer produced some copper coins from inside his robe, and they bought some food at a farmhouse. After Rafe recited his blessing upon the food, with proper praises of God, they feasted under the leaves of an old walnut tree, their first real food and drink since fleeing into the swamp. Then they rested and waited until after sunset.

"We'll be entering populated lands soon" the Seer said. "We can't afford to be seen, but don't let that darken your spirits. My father's a blacksmith who lives not far from here, and he'll provide us with everything we need."

At sunset, they rode on. The Seer seemed comforted by finding several more of Eric's glowing tracks shaded under thick overhanging branches; Karl and Rafe didn't seem happy to see them. Seren looked askance at the glowing marks that disappeared when a horse's hoof touched it; their vanishing didn't comfort her.

Late that night, as the bright moon rose amid the stars, they reached a crossroads beside a stream. They stopped, watered their horses, and Seren saw Karl staring at the nearly full moon, an odd expression masking his face.

"Why that look?" Seren asked.

Karl shrugged, almost smiling. "This is the same moon I was watching from the battlements of Castle Bristlen the day before Eric sailed into Demril. I'd been so cocky then, just a kid, and that was only a month ago.

My life wasn't peaceful, but I was content. Then Eric came, and Bristlen fell the night before the full moon, and my life's been insane ever since. If I told my father of the things I've seen since then, he'd call me mad."

"Me think mad, when see giant."

"Life is easier when you don't have to believe in magic."

Seren stifled a laugh. Living in brothels and taverns had taught her to recognize lies, even when the liar didn't know they were lying. Karl wasn't sad; he was subtly boasting that he'd seen more than his father, a triumph when perceived by one so young. Seren's eldest son had been the same at Karl's age.

Seren let Karl revel in his sensation of superiority. She'd seen his resoluteness mirrored on hundreds of young men, all trying to prove their prowess for two coppers, as if a whore would be impressed by their fumbling, newfound manhood. Seren smiled at Karl just as she'd smiled at all of those other young men. Let them preen and bristle their feathers; if Seren just laid back and looked interested then all men quickly tired and failed.

Rafe declared that their horses had drunk enough, and they mounted and rode on. Rafe and the Seer rode ahead, and Karl fell back to watch for pursuit, leaving Seren alone with the girls.

"Karl funny," Seren said.

Roselyn and Eloise, riding on opposite sides of her, snapped their heads to glare, and Seren knew she'd erred.

"Him young," she added.

Seren watched their expressions soften and relax. She'd known on sight that they were both Karl's lovers; the way they'd clung to him in the marketplace of Madrone revealed everything, but they were also aloof, playing young-girl games. In the swamp, she'd repeatedly overheard Karl inviting them, one at a time, to go for a walk, yet they'd always refused, and then teased him incessantly. The girls seemed to be allied against him, yet Seren noticed they always washed their arms slowly when Karl was nearby, and laughed playfully when he spoke. They weren't very good at it, but then, to Seren, attracting men was business. Yet Seren hadn't expected their fierce, protective stares when she mentioned Karl.

"Karl is ... dear to us," Roselyn said.

"Karl deer, you hunters," Seren said.

The women laughed.

"No more than you with Rafe," Eloise giggled.

"Rafe good man, hold Seren tight."

"Karl bad boy, hold no one," Roselyn said, and they all laughed again.

"Seren stay with Rafe," Seren said.

Conversation froze; Roselyn and Eloise fell silent, and Seren gazed knowingly at them. She shouldn't have mentioned staying; that inferred permanence, which Eloise and Roselyn didn't share while their rivalry lasted. Both were obviously in love with Karl, and best friends. Seren had seen many such situations; all ended poorly. Either their games would escalate until they drove Karl away, or Karl would choose one, and their friendship would end that minute.

Seren had listened to their discussions of sailing to France; both girls talked about a big house, and politely included her and the private room she'd share with Rafe. Yet they never spoke of where Karl would sleep, or who would share his bed. They couldn't both have him; they were fancy-born castle girls with rich fathers to spoil them, living carefree, easy lives of indulgence that brothel-born whores like Seren could only dream about. Yet eventually their man-sport would turn them against each other.

"Seer no ugly ... and powerful," Seren said.

Both women looked at her as if she were crazy.

Ah, youth! Seren chuckled silently. Tall and handsome was more attractive to young girls than more important qualities, like faithfulness and wealth. Still, Seren sensed that, if these girls separated, the company would quickly splinter, and that meant Rafe might go off alone. If Seren could divert the attentions of one girl away from Karl, it'd be better for her. The Seer was short, thin, and obnoxious, yet handsome and, more important, fair game.

Yet Rafe was her only concern. In the swamp, they'd gone for walks every day, even in the rain, once she'd gotten over The Shakes. Seren knew how easy men were to control, and how their belief in love could last forever ... as long as their needs were satisfied every day. Her trade-skills would bind Rafe to her, and she'd never fail to gratify him. If she could keep his feelings for her as strong as her feelings for him, then Rafe would always be hers.

Roselyn and Eloise rode on in silence. Seren glanced at their smooth, unwrinkled skin with no slight envy; Seren regretted that she was no longer young and pretty, but she appreciated the wisdom years of experience had given her. At least she didn't play love-games like these young girls.

Chapter 5

Disaster

KARL

Karl said nothing as they rode past the crumbling farmhouse where Rafe had stopped to warn the old peasants, not even when he saw a light inside their ramshackle hut. Eric had been with them then, and they'd been angry with him, but that seemed unimportant now.

Karl rode rearguard again. He occasionally looked behind; they were still in Sir Guldwin's lands, and if they were caught, then he wouldn't escape with just a lashing.

As the sun lowered across blue sky, Karl noticed the others were dismounting. His horse slowed as he approached.

"Are we stopping?" Karl asked.

"Roselyn and Eloise are nodding in their saddles," Rafe said, yawning. "I'm tired, too. We should rest here and ride up into the hills after dark. The Seer says there's a sheltered spot behind this ridge, under those trees, where we won't be seen from the road."

They found little shelter, just a small depression in the tall grass where deer had recently nested. They tied their horses with long tethers to small trees and threw their blankets, saddles, and shields over the grass. Their horse-blankets were sweat-damp; they'd been pressing their mounts hard, eager to get back into Eloise's lands.

As the sun fell, they ate half of their remaining provisions, then slept deeply.

Hours later, Karl awoke under a bright yellow moon. Looking about for signs of trouble, Karl spied Seren standing alone on a moonlit ridge. The others were sleeping soundly, Rafe snoring loudly, and Karl didn't want to disturb them. Yawning, he rose and walked toward Seren.

"Night forest beautiful," Seren said, "like Fairie."

"Titania you spoke of you knowing fairies as a child ...?" Karl asked.

"While Mama work, I into fields at night," Seren smiled. "Fairies find, watch while sleep. Trust Fairie, like trust you ... and Rafe."

"Rafe's a new man since he met you," Karl said.

"No, Rafe old man," Seren laughed, "but Rafe kindest I meet, and I meet many. Not need look farther."

Karl smiled; he was starting to like the old woman. Together they stared at the moon and stars.

The Seer awoke and roused the others. Rafe groaned loudly, and Roselyn threw a handful of damp grass at him. Eloise complained, demanding to be fed.

"Eat whatever we have left," the Seer said. "We'll get plenty soon."

They divided up the remainder of their provisions, mostly stale bread and old cheese, and passed around their last bottle of wine. Rafe ate quickly, then excused himself and walked off into the woods.

The wine tasted good, better than the bread and cheese, and Karl realized he appreciated tastes more after their detention in the swamp. They finished off every scrap of food and drained the last bottle before they gave thought to leaving.

Suddenly a loud 'thunk' echoed nearby. Karl froze, recognizing the chop of a metal sword, although he could see little through the dark trees.

"Rafe ...!" Karl shouted.

Karl jumped up and dashed in the direction of the echo, drawing his sword as he stumbled through dark woods. Anyone could be out here in the wild, and Rafe was alone …!

Another swordblow crashed. Karl raced toward it.

Finally Karl spied Rafe, sword raised against a towering menace, and Karl charged to help.

Suddenly Karl stopped; Rafe was standing alone, naked sword in his hand, facing a tree. Rafe swung and struck the tree with his sword; the loud chop echoed.

"Rafe, what are you doing …?"

"Trying to learn to use this thing," Rafe said, wrenching his blade from the scored tree. "I liked my pitchfork better."

"Why …?"

"This company survived before because we had two great fighters, you and Eric," Rafe said. "Now Eric's gone. We still need two fighters, and I don't trust the Seer like the rest of you."

"Trust the Seer …?" Karl laughed. "I'd hand him over to Sir Guldwin myself!"

Both men laughed, yet Rafe quickly fell silent. He looked down, and Karl sighed.

"Rafe, I can teach you how to fight with a sword," Karl said. "I'm no King's Champion like Eric, but …"

"What am I doing wrong …?" Rafe asked.

Karl paused, considering. Rafe was different than he, shorter and heavier. Different body types had to fight differently; Rafe couldn't just mimic Karl's style. Yet some basics that never changed.

"Fighting with a sword is more than swinging steel," Karl said. "It's attitude, determination to win. Nothing else matters. There're tricks you can use, but most fighters know them, so you can't rely on tricks. You have to be the victor in your mind before the fight begins."

"Okay," Rafe said eagerly.

Karl looked at his old friend; Rafe didn't yet understand, but that didn't matter. You couldn't learn fighting from words, and you couldn't learn a few movements and expect to win a real fight.

Good fighting requires experience. Karl had grown up fighting his brothers with sticks. He knew his best motions; a combination of ten or eleven moves, the more unexpected, the better. Facing equal opponents, the one who could surprise the other would most-likely win.

The middle of a fight is too late to learn; either you already know how to fight or you die. Teaching a beginner was dangerous; if any fighter overestimated their ability even once, then they died.

Karl showed Rafe how to stand balanced, and how to lead his sword-swings with his hips and put all his weight into each blow. Rafe kept swinging wide or sticking his elbow out, where it could get struck by an opponent's blade, yet Karl broke a thin branch off the tree and began hitting Rafe where he was making mistakes. He showed Rafe three shots: at the neck, at the leg, and how to swing over his head to the other side.

"What're you doing ...?" Eloise asked, and both turned to discover the others had found them.

"Karl and I are practicing," Rafe said. "Well, he's teaching."

"We have to go," the Seer said.

"In a minute," Karl said.

The Seer scowled and walked away.

Karl went and stood behind the trunk of the tree, telling Rafe to attack him slowly. Rafe tried, yet Karl easily ducked behind the trunk, avoiding his swings. Then Karl reached around the tree and tapped Rafe with his stick.

"Look for things to hide behind as you fight," Karl said. "Until you get more experienced, try to fight from behind cover as much as you can."

Karl began drilling Rafe in the three basic attacks: head, leg, and over your head to your opponent's other side. The exaggerated postures of fighting were uncomfortable at first, yet Rafe managed, and soon Karl pulled out his sword and they began fighting in slow motion, moving in wide, over-balanced movements. In the poor light, they had to go very slowly to keep from killing each other.

"Pretend you're swimming," Karl said. "Move like you're underwater, pushing against the current. And don't watch my face."

Suddenly Karl grinned wide, showing all of his teeth. Rafe froze and stared at him, and Karl turned his swinging blade and stopped it only an inch from Rafe's wide nose.

"Watch my sword, not my face," Karl laughed. "Many fighters'll try to distract you by doing weird things; distraction on a battlefield means death."

The Seer called for them again, and they sheathed their swords.

"You should start wearing your shield instead of letting it hang from your saddle," Karl said as they walked back to their horses. "The only way to get used to the weight of a shield is to wear it."

"I have Eric's helm, but I could use a coat of rings like yours," Rafe said.

"Wear the helm," Karl said. "Armor took me a while to get used to, but I barely feel it now. We'll be in Eloise's lands tonight; maybe she can get you some mail. We'll continue sword-practicing each time we stop."

Rafe clapped Karl on his back; Karl winced under his blow. Rafe instantly apologized: both of their backs were still tender from Guldwin's whips.

Their long ride uphill was hard, the slopes far steeper than Karl remembered, but then he'd been riding downhill. His heavy shield was strapped to him arm again, as Rafe's was, but Rafe was soon struggling to keep from poking his horse with the square edges of his larger shield, and eventually Rafe just let his left arm hang. Karl understood; holding a shield takes lots of practice. After a few hours from Bristlen, Karl's arm had begun to cramp, but he'd said nothing, as he knew Rafe would say nothing, because of pride.

They stopped for a rest halfway up the slope, their horses strained and salivating. Rafe went from horse to horse, and poured water into his hand to let them drink, while the others stood and stretched. Then Rafe wiped his hands clean and drew his sword. Karl turned Rafe to face a tree, corrected his stance, and Rafe swung.

The sun rose as they rode higher. Their path seemed arduous; Karl rode rearguard closer than usual. He heard Eloise and Seren laughing, yet Roselyn rode alone, silently ahead of them.

The ashes were long cold as they rode into view of ruined Grusshire. Every building was gone; only strangely familiar skeletons of charred beams haunted where once stood houses and barns of a peaceful village. Burned-stink filled the air, even at a distance, dusting their lips with a bitter, acrid taste. Karl bowed his head in shame; Grusshire was nothing but ashes, and they were to blame.

"Oh, Gods of Evil ...!" the Seer cried. *"What happened ...? What happened to Grusshire ...? Oh, Gods ...!"*

The Seer spurred to a gallop and rode madly ahead. Roselyn shouted, then spurred after him. Karl frowned; trouble had come.

He, Rafe, and Eloise exchanged nervous glances, and then spurred and chased their companions all the way into the blackened corpse of Grusshire.

Alone, Roselyn sat atop her horse, still as stone, staring in horror at the awful sight.

The Seer knelt on the stone steps of the burned out blacksmith's shop, and suddenly Karl recalled where he'd seen the Seer's coal-black hair and eyes before. He knew what had become of the blacksmith's absent son. Tears streamed from the Seer's eyes as he clenched the broken haft of a Viking pike.

"Dead ...!" the Seer cried. *"My parents are dead ...! Damn those Vikings! Damn their race to eternal torment! Goddess, damn their souls! Tear their dead from rest and hurl them from existence! Strike your wintry storms upon them! Slay them with your summer bolts! Oh, Gods! Mother ...! Father ...! Forgive me ...! I didn't know ...!"*

A long moment passed. Seren glanced at the rest of them, and finally she dismounted and hurried to the Seer. She embraced him, but darted questioning looks back at the stunned companions. Karl hung in his saddle, swaying between dismay and disbelief. Roselyn sat ashen white. Rafe bowed and prayed, and Eloise started to cry.

With a guttural scream, Roselyn turned and spurred to a gallop, back the way that they'd come.

"Help Seren ...!" Karl cried, spurring hard after Roselyn.

His stallion reared, and then raced through Roselyn's dust. He had to catch her; at this speed, she could kill herself if she plunged over the ridge. Perhaps her horse would stop, refuse to descend at a gallop, yet Karl couldn't take that chance.

Roselyn's mare was fast, but Eric's powerful warhorse quickly closed the distance. Just as they approached the crest, Karl pulled abreast, and he wrapped an arm around Roselyn and lifted her from saddle and horse. She struggled to push free, but Karl clung with desperate strength, carefully slowed his horse to a halt, and slid to the ground still holding her.

"Roselyn, stop!" Karl shouted. "You can't undo what's been done!"

"What's been done ...?" Roselyn cried. "What we did, you mean! *We killed his parents ...!"*

"No! Remember ...? We sent the women away, in the cart. His mother should still be alive."

"So we only killed his father, his friends, and his village ...!"

"Svenson would've come this way anyway," Karl said, though he knew it was a pitiful excuse. "It's the only road through the hills."

"We could've warned them!" Roselyn cried. "We could've helped! We could've died with them!

What are we, riding laughing, while innocents die at our backs?"

"We were fighting for our lives, running from an army! Remember Bristlen and Demril? Svenson's army killed everyone in Othar, village and castle! They probably killed Baron du Harmonn in his bed! Us they would have killed slowly, each pain lasting days!"

"We killed them ...! We killed them all ...!"

Roselyn crumbled and fell sobbing into Karl's arms.

"We're lost ...! Lost ...!"

"No, Roselyn," Karl whispered, trying to comfort her. "I don't know ... what came over us. It seems so long ago. It was like ... Eric carried a magic, enchanting us with all our fancy weapons and treasure. We forgot ourselves. We forgot everything."

Roselyn sobbed and Karl held her tightly.

"We have to go back," Karl said, "before the Seer finds out."

Roselyn nodded, yet for long moments she held fast to him.

"Roselyn, maybe this is a blessing," Karl said carefully.

"What ...?" Roselyn looked shocked.

"The Seer," Karl explained. "He won't want to travel with us anymore, and we never asked to travel with him. We're out of Sir Guldwin's lands. Maybe it's time we sailed to France and ended this stupid quest."

"What about Eric ...?"

"Do you really believe Eric is making those yellow tracks?"

"Who else ...?"

"Killing ourselves won't help Eric," Karl reached out his hand, caressed her hair, and pulled her close. "Come away with me, just the two of us. We'll find a ship, get passage to France."

"What about the others?"

"They'll be fine."

"We can't just leave them ..."

"You promised me anything," Karl reminded her. "Remember ...? When I rode back alone, to save Eric ...?"

"Karl, no ..."

"You promised ...!"

Roselyn bowed her head.

"Not ... yet," she whispered, and Roselyn pulled away.

Karl and Roselyn gathered their horses and rode back slowly. They dreaded facing the Seer. Nothing could excuse their crime; the Seer couldn't forgive them.

They rode into fallen Grusshire to find their companions hard at work. Rafe, Eloise, and Seren stood around a new, shallow hole dug just off the road, in the remains of a wide goose-pen in front of the blacksmith's house. Eloise, Seren, and the Seer had shovels in their hands. Rafe had a pick; all were digging, widening the hole.

Confused, Karl dismounted, then helped Roselyn down. Rafe paused to look at him, a serious, cold stare full of warning, and then he nodded to a small pile of hoes and other digging tools.

Trusting Rafe, Karl said nothing. He just selected a pick like Rafe had, save that its handle was charred on one side, and slid in between Eloise and Seren. Karl swung his pick with practiced hands and broke up huge clods of dirt, which the girls quickly removed with their shovels. Karl didn't know why he was digging, yet farm chores were no stranger to him, and he'd rather dig up all of ruined Grusshire than explain why he'd ruined it.

Around noon, Eloise dropped her shovel and staggered away. Karl seized the opportunity to share her break, mumbled something about water, and followed Eloise.

"What're we digging for ...?" Karl whispered when no one but Eloise could hear.

"A grave," Eloise whispered back. "For the men of Grusshire. Vikings piled their bodies in the smithy before they burned the town. The Seer said we can't leave them unburied, and he gathered these tools, began digging, and hasn't said another word since. Karl, what'll make my hands stop hurting?"

"Live on a farm for five years," Karl answered. "Did he find his father's bones?"

"All Grusshire is under that fallen roof, over a hundred charred skeletons."

"How did he take the news ...?"

Eloise bowed her head.

"He doesn't know," Eloise said. "But he's a Seer; what we don't tell him, he'll find out."

Karl's frown deepened. *How powerful was the Seer, and what could they do if he turned against them? What tactics worked against magic?*

Even the Seer was too exhausted to work straight through the afternoon, and soon after everyone quit. Eloise, Roselyn and Seren had sore, aching muscles and cracked, swollen hands. Karl and Rafe fared little better; the fresh scars on their backs stung and ached.

Their new hole was now a wide pit, four feet deep, big enough for all of them to stand in. The Seer sat upon the ground before the wide pit, his shovel cast aside, clenching a broken Viking pike-shaft as if drawing power from it.

Karl fretted, wondering how much power he was drawing ... and what he'd do with it.

Slowly the sun sank below the horizon, and a clear, starlit sky illuminated shadowy, charred ruins. The Seer sat unmoving, staring without blinking. Karl felt worried; the full moon would be rising soon, and it boded ill on such nights for the living to disturb the dead.

The Seer began to sing.

The Seer sang as if he were a corpse, unmoving save for a slight twitching of his barely open mouth, staring glassily forward, a low, mournful drone that filled the quiet night air. He sang a funeral chant, no words, but a haunting, desolate melody.

Long they sat and waited, shivering in the chill wind that rose as if in response to the Seer's song. Eloise clutched fearfully at Karl's left arm, Roselyn at his right. Rafe held Seren in respectful silence.

Wood began to crackle across the street from the smoky ruin where the skeletons laid. A great column of black soot wafted up from the villager's ashen tomb, yet no light from a fire showed. Shadowed figures wandered about inside its black cloud. As one they emerged, slowly walking out of the ruin into the pale, ghostly light.

Karl's eyes widened.

The dead of Grusshire walked out of the ruin, charred corpses and blackened bones staggering as if cursed with a false life. They walked with slow, jerking movements. Many dragged crushed or broken appendages, and some had limbs missing. They moved like obscene puppets to the cadence of the Seer's chant. A few dragged legless torsos across the dirt.

Each tried to scream, yet voices caught in every throat. The wave of horror emerged into the starlight and stood before the yawning pit.

As the skeletons reached the edge of the pit, their walking bones halted. Finally the Seer ceased his dreadful song and looked at them.

"Why have you stopped?" the Seer asked. "Here lies your welcome grave, eternal rest, instead of endless haunting. Enter, and be at peace."

The living skeletons stood unmoving in the silent starlight. Then fierce and terrible skulls turned to face the companions. Black-charred hands lifted to point bony fingers.

Everyone screamed.

"Seer, send them back ...!" Rafe shouted. "By God in Heaven, send them back ...!"

"I won't let my father rot in unhallowed ground!" the Seer cried. "What's the meaning of this? Why do they point at you?"

"We rode through Grusshire, hours before the Vikings ...!" Karl shouted. "We helped them fortify their town ...!"

"Farmers fight Vikings ...?" the Seer gasped.

"Eric led us," Karl fumbled for words. "We were ... drunk with his vision of glory, chased by the whole Viking army! We tried to help them!"

"What evil did you do ...?" the Seer demanded.

"We tricked them ...!" Rafe shouted suddenly, releasing Seren and falling to his knees. "God forgive us! We deceived them about the Viking's numbers! We conned them into putting up a hopeless defense to cover our escape! God Almighty ...! Slay me for my sins! Why did we do it ...?"

The Seer glared, frozen, but furious eyes blazed. He made no movement or sign, and Karl glanced from the Seer to the walking skeletons, and wondered which was the greater terror. Then the Seer began to sing again.

The Seer's new song sounded identical to his first, slow and haunting, yet harsher, pounding like a deep drum.

Suddenly the skeletons moved, slow bones rattling. Animated bones turned to both sides, and began marching around the pit.

"Seer, no ...!" Karl cried, but to no avail.

Karl swept out his sword to rush the Seer, yet living skeletons stepped between them. Karl fell back, pushing the girls as he went.

"Rafe, get up ...!" Karl shouted. *"Rafe ...!"*

Pulling Rafe by the arm, Karl drug him off his knees, to his feet. Everyone was screaming.

"Hurry!" Karl shouted to the others. *"Get out of here!"*

Karl glanced to where they'd left the horses tethered: their horses were gone, probably fled when the skeletons first appeared.

Karl pushed frantically, and together he, Rafe, Roselyn, Eloise, and Seren ran west down the main street toward the ruin of the large barricade.

"Murderers ...!" the Seer cried. *"Parent-killers ...! Were your few lives worth the generations that died here? Now you will fear Athelwynne the Seer ...!"*

They reached the end of the road. Before the burned, fallen barricade, a high mound of dirt had been raised. Desperate, Karl didn't even pause to wonder, thinking only that they could hide on the other side of it.

Suddenly the tall, dirt mound began to crumble.

Putrefying hands and insect-ridden arms, still clenching steel weapons, pushed through the piled earth, digging free. Karl looked back to see the Seer standing in the middle of the road, his arms raised to the sky, singing his dead-summoning song to a new, fevered cadence.

"A Viking burial mound ...!" Rafe cried.

Karl froze, disbelieving; the Seer was summoning forth the Viking dead, who also hated them, to aid the charred skeletons of Grusshire.

Karl dragged Eloise and Roselyn, still screaming, to one side, searching franticly for a passage through the fallen, burned-out houses entrapping them, when the first of the rotting Vikings pulled free.

"Rafe, draw your sword!" Karl shouted. *"We're going to have to fight our way out! Girls, get behind us!"*

Seren, Roselyn, and Eloise drew back, terrified, quaking. Rafe drew his sword. They backed away from the armed Vikings in front of them, but that forced them back toward the approaching skeletons.

Karl saw fear in Rafe's eyes. He'd have to act first, and boldly, or they'd fail. Yet Karl's legs felt weak as a child's. The wave of skeletons crept ever closer; Karl's revulsion grew, yet he couldn't falter. Teeth clenched, Karl raised his sword and charged.

Charred skeletons shattered pitifully as he struck, many toppling over. His sword cleaved through eerie ranks like a heavy axe through dried twigs. Blackened skulls smashed, limbs flew apart, and ribs exploded in clouds of deathly ash. Karl fought as a titan; his enemies stumbled into range mindless of the destruction of their fellows. Karl clove deep into their midst; he could take on them all ... if his strength held out.

A grip of iron seized his shoulder. A skeletal hand closed around his throat. Karl choked under its squeeze, unable to breathe. Another grip, stronger than any mortal possessed, clamped onto his shield. Fiercely Karl twisted, flailing with his sword. Karl sheared the charred arm from the hand that held his neck, yet its grisly fist held fast.

More bony fingers reached for him, but Karl had to ignore them, desperate to breathe. He pounded his sword's pommel against his neck, smashing the bony fingers crushing his throat until they shattered into dust. But even as Karl gasped life, more hands, more claws of death, reached for him. Karl tried to fight, but blackened finger-bones clutched his arms, and Karl was lifted like a helpless child.

Screaming, Karl thrashed wildly. Thoughts flooded of being carried to the huge grave he'd helped dig, of being laid in it, crushed and surrounded by his morbid pallbearers, buried alive under the overwhelming weight of Grusshire's vengeful dead.

I earned this death, Karl thought. *I'm a traitor, a murderer of my own Saxon race.*

"Karl ...!" Rafe screamed above the din, throwing his weight against the skeletons holding Karl aloft. The pack stumbled as Roselyn ran up with a charred wooden

board, smashing into the press, with Eloise and Seren close behind her.

Roselyn berserked, madly swinging her club directly at the knees of every skeleton closing in behind them as they pushed toward Karl through the wall of thrashing, crawling bones. Karl glimpsed a fell light in Roselyn's eyes that startled him, despite their predicament. Rafe thrashed the skeletons holding Karl, fervently swinging his sword through their midst until they dropped him, and Seren and Eloise began pulling severed limbs from Karl, and finally broke him free.

Karl gasped, spared, but only for the moment.

"We've got to find Athelwynne!" Roselyn cried. *"Only he can stop this!"*

Weakly Karl banged his sword on the ground to break off the still-clenching hands, when a horrible sound made him look up. Under the light of the brilliant stars and the almost-risen full moon, Karl saw a horror to freeze his blood: through the ashen smoke of stumbling skeletons marched Viking corpses, growling horribly through rotting throats, smashing and stamping to dust everything that stood between them. These zombies wielded not brittle skeletal hands but swords of tempered steel, axes of beaten iron; the weapons they'd been buried with.

Seren screamed.

"Fight ...!" Rafe shouted. "Karl, fight! Drive our way to the Seer! Attack the bones of Grusshire!"

"Take the lead!" Karl shouted, still gasping.

Karl staggered. His limbs felt like iron under the weight of his armor, and he was so tired he could barely stand. Rafe struck at the remaining wall of skeletons like a holy crusader, Roselyn on his right with her club. Together they opened a gap.

The full moon rose to its brightest to illuminate a scene from darkest hell.

"Karl ...!" Eloise cried, wrapping an arm about him. "Are you hurt? Come on! We've got to help ...!"

Eloise raised her head to face the night sky ... and her words caught in her throat. Suddenly Eloise fell to the ground and vomited. Karl shook the weariness from his limbs and reached to assist her: no one could fault Eloise for being sick on this battlefield. Yet she wouldn't rise.

"Eloise, hurry ...!" Karl shouted.

Vikings marched within spear-reach.

Quickly Karl hacked at a spearhaft, dragging Eloise out of their reach, screaming for her to run, but Eloise only convulsed harder and choked back a scream.

Karl picked her up and started to carry her. *If only he could reach the Seer!* Karl would make him stop this, or he'd kill him. Yet, in the thick ashen mist, Karl couldn't even see the Seer.

Eloise thrashed violently, broke free from Karl's grasp, and fell onto the road. Viking corpses approached closer. Horrible under the risen full moon, they stank of the grave, yet Karl couldn't let them kill Eloise; Karl charged the Viking dead.

Spearheads he brushed aside, and Karl threw a mighty blow at the foremost of the dead Vikings. His steel sword split the Viking's head in two. But to Karl's horror, the deadly wound neither slew nor slowed the Viking.

The dead Viking raised its notched, broken sword and hacked at Karl. Barely Karl dodged it, when he realized that his sword was stuck in the zombie's split head. Karl pulled hard to free his sword, yet another dead Viking swung at him, and Karl had to flee, barehanded, as the grimy corpses lumbered forward.

Falling back, Karl tripped over Eloise, still screaming in agony, writhing on the ground.

Karl threw himself over her, protecting Eloise with his life, when a stout spear stabbed forward and caught his mailed chest. Protected by his steel rings, Karl fell backwards onto a pile of twitching, broken bones. Karl scrambled to his feet and raised his head only to see a broken sword strike home on Eloise's shoulder, slicing deep into her neck. Karl screamed as Eloise did, but he could only watch as Eloise fell twitching, blood spurting from her wound.

Karl jumped barehanded at the rotting Vikings, ready to rend Viking flesh with his bare hands, when a black smoke burst up from the ground between them, and a stench only Hell could equal drove Karl and the Vikings apart.

Eloise rolled onto her back, convulsing, and suddenly she howled like a wolf. Claws stabbed out of her soft, slender fingertips. Eloise's mouth stretched outwards into a short muzzle. Fangs burst through gums. Blonde hair erupted from Eloise's pale skin ... until golden fur covered her face and hands. Blue eyes of innocence darkened to red orbs of hate.

A female figure stood, Eloise no longer. Eloise had transformed, her shape revealing its cause: *although they'd slain him and saved her, the curse of the Wolflord had returned ...!*

Karl fell back, overcome at last. He fell to his knees and sobbed like a pitiful child. Eloise glared at Karl, red eyes flaming, fang-filled muzzle snarling, claws ready to tear him to pieces. Karl never moved; he couldn't fight Eloise, not even to defend his life.

A Viking sword stabbed Eloise from behind. Eloise turned and leapt full upon her attacker, her evil-wrought fangs and claws sinking deep into dead Viking flesh as her growls filled the dusty air.

Karl sat frozen, stunned, watching Hell fight itself; Eloise's claws tore into the Viking corpse with a vengeance. With unbelievable strength, Eloise ripped its head from its shoulders; the Viking body collapsed. Grisly seconds later, another undead Viking fell, rended; the Viking corpse Karl had thought unslayable lay shredded at Eloise's feet, a stinking pile of slashed flesh, indistinguishable save for Karl's precious sword still buried in its severed head.

Quickly Eloise pounced on another Viking and ripped it apart in a flurry of claws and savagery. The corpses attacked Eloise, but their slow, heavy blows Eloise easily dodged, and those that landed had as little effect on her as Eric and Karl's swords had on the Wolflord.

Swinging from nowhere, an axe split Eloise's skull wide open, and Karl screamed as Eloise fell. The Vikings lumbered toward her, chopping, rending her strange corpse. Then suddenly a black mist burst from the ground. Karl actually laughed, a weak, insane chuckle.

Fur-clad, Eloise rose whole and strong, angrier than before, and attacked with renewed savagery.

Eloise vanished into the press of dead Vikings, yet her shrill howls and the sounds of ripping claws told Karl that she needed no help.

A lone, stumbling, rickety skeleton loomed out of the ashen mist, shaking Karl from his reverie. As it approached, Karl glared at it like a bow being slowly drawn. Karl jumped to his feet; its skull flew off from Karl's punch. Karl grabbed its ribs with his left hand and lifted it into the air, shaking it. It was surprisingly light; Karl threw it down and stomped it into dust. Eyeing his fallen sword, he snatched for its grip, pried it from the severed Viking head, and ran into the small press of skeletons that were left.

Nothing stopped him. Karl felt transformed, as if he'd become the fighting animal from Hell. Bones flew before his sword. Karl laughed as he slew, and before he knew it, no more skeletons stood, only

Roselyn staring at him like he was mad. Rafe seized hold of Karl from behind and shouted in his ear.

"Karl ...! Stop! It's over! They're gone!"

"Karl ...?" Roselyn asked. "Where's Eloise ...?"

Karl stared horrified at Roselyn; *what could he say?*

Roselyn's face twisted with grief.

"On, no ...!" Roselyn shouted. *"Not Eloise ...!"*

"No ...," Karl stammered. "She's ... Eloise's ... not ... dead ...!"

"Where is she ...?" Rafe shouted in his ear. *"If she's hurt ...!"*

"No," Karl said, his voice failing. "We can't help. Eloise is ... lost. We're too late: a month late. A month, Rafe! One cycle of the moon! *The Wolflord ... cursed her ...! Eloise is gone!"*

Rafe stared, then pushed Karl aside and ran back towards the Vikings. Karl dashed after him, with Roselyn following. They found Rafe standing just outside a ring of piles of slain Vikings.

Eloise, recognizable only by the shreds of her red dress and her long fall of blonde hair, was fighting still. Viking zombies mindlessly attacked her, unaware that their weapons had no effect.

Rafe and Roselyn stood dumbfounded. Karl slowly pulled them back, away from the fight, before they became her prey.

"This is the evilest of nights," Rafe said, and he crossed himself. "The devil himself has doomed us."

"Eloise ...!" Roselyn sobbed. *"We have to ...!"*

"She'll kill us if she sees us," Karl said.

"She wouldn't harm us!" Rafe argued.

"Eloise wouldn't," Karl said, "but look at her! Is that beast our princess? I watched her die before she changed, and still she rose to fight! While the full moon lasts, Eloise won't know us!"

"Athelwynne ...!" Roselyn snarled. "Where is he? He'll save her ... or I'll cut out his heart!"

"Yes," Rafe agreed. "Let's find the Seer!"

Chapter 6

Hopeless and Helpless

SEREN

Seren ran through clouds of flying ash, leaving the others to finish off the skeletons. She's last seen the Seer by the open grave, but he wasn't there. Seren stared about, scanning the burned-out ruins of Grusshire, and then spied an odd shape ... lying at the bottom of the grave. Seren hesitated; entering an open grave was a bad omen, yet Seren clenched her teeth and climbed in.

The Seer laid sprawled face-down in the dirt, despite the bright moon, his black robes hidden in shadow. Seren rolled his cold body over and brushed dirt from his face. He'd brought the dead to life; *only he could send them back.*

"Holy Mary, make him live," Seren prayed.

"Blessed Lady, take me now," the Seer moaned.

"Seer ...!" Seren shouted. *"You alive! Wake up!"*

"Too tired," the Seer mumbled. "Magic ... drained. Need sleep."

"No!" Seren cried. *"Dead after us! You turn back!"*

"Can't. Too weak."

Seren drew back her hand and slapped the Seer.

"Wake up, you filthy murdering liced bastard villain-priest ...! You conjure ...! Kill now! End spell!"

"No way ... to stop," the Seer said. "Spirits ... united with shells. Natural. Shells must be broken. I've pushed limits ... exhausted. Must rest."

"Now ...!" Seren cried, and she raised her fisted and hammered it between the Seer's robed thighs. A pain-retching scream choked and gagged as he jerked and rolled, clutching his groin and gasping.

"You do this!" Seren cried. *"Help now, or I crack you like egg! Friends in trouble!"*

"Friends ....?" The Seer cried. *"What about my friends ...? My family ...?!?"*

"Killing us no help!"

"Justice ...!" the Seer cried. "Horned one, give me strength! Murder must be avenged!"

"Why?" Seren demanded. "So village folk rest? You no one to speak! We ride in, dead gone to reward!

You disturb dead! For hate, you bring dead back, break dead's peace!"

"I loved them ...!"

"Village folk good. Fight to save homes, die well. Afterlife be good. Now Seer call good people back to kill, send to graves with bloody hands! Seer make good parents murderers! What reward be for murderers? Hellfire! Punishment always! Good people hate and curse Seer forever!"

"My parents are dead ...!!!" the Seer shouted right in Seren's face, yet her countenance remained hard and severe, stiff-lipped. As she stared back at him, the Seer's grief broke like a wave upon rocks.

"Gone ...! Murdered ...! I can't forget ...!"

Seren pulled him close, cradling the Seer like a babe.

"Never forget," Seren promised. "Not know Eric long, but no believe him evil. Give others chance to explain. Parents understand. Stop dead now, send back to grave. I help."

"I ... I can't," sobbed the Seer. "It's a spell of awakening, irreversible, and I'm too weak to undo a complex conjuring."

"Then come," Seren said. "We do what can."

"All right," the Seer sobbed. "But I want a full accounting ...!"

"Me want, too," Seren said seriously. "But now not time. I hope can still find ..."

Suddenly the companions burst in on them, jumping into the grave, and knocking them over.

"Hey ...!" Seren shouted. *"Watch out!"*

"Seer!" Karl cried, grabbing the Seer and pulling him close. "You've got to stop Eloise!"

"Get your hands off me ...!!" the Seer slapped Karl away.

Karl drew back and raised his sword.

"Karl, no!" Seren cried, and she jumped between them. "No have that now!"

"Seer, please ...!" Roselyn begged, and she fell onto her knees before the Seer. "Whatever else, you must save Eloise!"

"Please," Rafe added, "or we'll have to kill her."

"Save ...?" Seren asked. "Eloise hurt ...?"

"Cursed," Karl said, and he pointed into the ashen mists.

The Seer and Seren exchanged confused looks, then stood up and peered out at fallen Grusshire. The dirt road lay paved in pale, twitching, moonlit bones covered by an ashen fog. In the distance, Viking zombies pressed in a circle, swords raised. From inside their circle rose a terrible howl. Suddenly a blonde figure leaped up into the moonlight, more wolf than human, with a long fall of blonde hair down its back, wearing shreds of Eloise's long red dress. It ... *Eloise* ... fell upon the attacking Vikings with fangs and claws ... like demons carved on the tops of cathedrals.

The Seer gasped.

Seren fainted.

Chapter 7

The Taming of a Werewolf

RAFE

The full moon faded as the sun rose. Long yellow-leafed willow branches swayed overhead, and green grasses grew tall around them, as Rafe held Seren. Rafe leaned back against a willow trunk and stared at the distant ruins of Grusshire in the sunlight, relieved that the horrid night was over.

"No ...!" Seren screamed as she awakened, yet Rafe held her firmly, protectively.

"It's morning, my love. It's over."

"But ... but Eloise ...!"

"The Seer says she'll be all right ... human, now that the sun's up. Nothing could hurt her last night ... and we'll protect her now."

"What ... *how ...?"*

"The Wolflord, a devil that kidnapped Eloise as we fled from Castle Bristlen," Rafe said. "We didn't know, but she continues his curse. While the full moon shines each month, she'll ... transform ... become a wolf-thing."

"Seer no leave ...?" Seren asked.

"Only because he failed to kill us. He's been more himself than usual; snapping, yelling, or just ignoring us; I can't blame him."

"Why no ...?"

"We killed his whole town ... and his father," Rafe said. "We followed Eric too far, to save our own lives, and it just ... got out of hand. We left this town to be slaughtered by Svenson's Vikings. We didn't know ..."

Seren sat up, pushed free of Rafe's arms, and stared as if seeing him with a new eyes. Rafe bowed his head.

"I don't blame you," Rafe said. "It was ... unforgivable, and I can't endure the guilt. But once Eric started it, we couldn't stop; they'd have killed us."

Seren stared long at Rafe, grimly frowning; her disapproving glare burned.

"What plan now?" Seren asked.

"I don't know," Rafe admitted. "First, we find Eloise and get her settled. Then Karl wants to have a meeting ... to explain everything."

"How settle Eloise ...?"

"I don't know," Rafe said. "Perhaps the Seer can help. But Eloise is part of our company; I won't forsake her."

In the distance, from behind the ruins of Grusshire, Karl appeared, Eloise naked in his arms, sobbing. Roselyn walked beside him, holding Eloise's head. Eloise was human again, all shreds of her red dress gone, yet without a scratch or blemish.

When Karl reached them, Rafe rose and untied a cloak from his saddle to cover and comfort Eloise, but in vain; Eloise blubbered and heeded nothing. Karl leaned his mailed-back against a nearby maple, and then slid down it to sit, still holding Eloise. Roselyn whispered comforting words, but Rafe doubted if Eloise even heard.

Slowly the Seer walked up. A disgusted expression twisted his face, and he spat on the ground.

"Nothing we can say ...," Rafe started.

"Still your murderous tongue ...!" the Seer shouted. "If I didn't need you for the Lady's quest ...!"

"You almost killed us last night," Rafe reminded.

"Your deaths were justified," the Seer snapped. "But the Lady needs you ... so I won't kill you ... yet."

"Cure Eloise and we'll do anything you say," Roselyn promised.

"Lycanthropy is an ancient evil, more powerful than some gods; no Druid wields such power. Silver alone can kill Eloise; it's her only escape."

Eloise burst into tears, and Rafe glared at the Seer.

"There must be some way," Rafe said to Eloise. "We will find it. I promise."

"What about Grusshire ...?" the Seer demanded. "Don't lie; I'll know."

"Eric," Karl explained. "Well, mostly Eric. We were following him, like we're following you. He didn't tell us what he was planning, just like you're not telling us where ..."

"Don't make excuses!"

"You didn't know Eric like we did," Karl said. "Eric mastered and commanded. He lied with an ease I couldn't believe, and tricked people better than illusions. Eric walked in to Bristlen to rob it, with lies, and they rolled out the carpet for him, fed him, and gave him a bed. He slaughtered Bristlen the night he sailed here, in pretty much the same way he made Grusshire fall; he told people what they wanted to hear."

"What did he tell them?"

"That the main Viking army had turned back, and only a few hundred renegades remained," Karl said. "Your townsmen chose to defend their homes, and by then it was too late; they would've killed us."

"So you let them die ...?"

"It was a mistake," Rafe said. "We realized it too late. We were angry, too."

"Blame me," Roselyn said. "I could've spoken, but didn't."

"No," Eloise whimpered. "I-I'm their baroness; I-I'm why they listened ..."

"You I might spare," the Seer said to Eloise. "Your curse is a more fitting punishment than any I could devise. Unfortunately, the Lady needs you all; She alone is keeping you alive."

"That's not the whole truth," Karl said, clutching Eloise protectively. "You need to know everything."

Karl told their whole tale, of the day Eric sailed into the harbor below Othar and how Eric forced him to rob the treasury of Castle Bristlen, of how they met Roselyn and Eloise, and how Rafe helped them escape as Svenson Two-Sword arrived, leading his Viking army to siege the castle.

The Seer never moved or interrupted, just stood unblinking, hate masking his face. Rafe noted that Seren was also listening intently, her expression equally displeased.

Rafe took over, telling of the wolf attack on the Baron's hunting lodge, Eloise's abduction, their long search, Liz Apple's sudden appearance, and of his slaying of the Wolflord. Eloise shuddered in Karl's lap, whimpering all the while. Roselyn tried to comfort her, but to little avail. Rafe sympathized, fearing that his words would only increase Eloise's misery, so he quickly finished his tale.

Roselyn quickly took up the story to change the topic. Roselyn told how they spent the night at Farmer Tiller's house, of the thieves that ambushed them on the road, of their meeting with Svenson's scouts, and how they rode into Grusshire with an army on their heels. At this the Seer visibly froze, ceasing all apparent movement, even breathing; he just stared at Roselyn.

Openly, as if to a confessor, Roselyn told the Seer everything they did, even vague impressions and private feelings. Roselyn rambled on, detail after detail, until ...

"Let Roselyn go ...!" Seren snapped irritably. "Being honest. No trial trust."

The Seer relaxed, averted his stare, and Roselyn swooned. Rafe caught and steadied Roselyn as she shook her head and winced, as if awakening from a long sleep.

Curtly Rafe finished the story, specifically detailing how he helped load the women and children, and a few elder men, in a big cart, and sent them away before the battle began. Then he described their anger at Eric after they rode out. Rafe started telling how they stopped to shout warnings at every farmhouse, yet the Seer interrupted him.

"Enough," the Seer said. "You've admitted your guilt. Your excuses fail. Why I should forgive you?"

"No one asked for forgiveness, sorcerer," Rafe said. "If you want compensation, we'll consider it. But don't lord over us as if you're our master. We're free companions, to come and go as we choose. You forced your company upon us, remember?"

"Eric ... believed he was helping those farmers by making them warriors," Karl said. "He believed they were chosen by Valkyrie and carried to Valhalla; not only them, but also those Vikings they killed. You never heard Eric boast of his faith, Seer, and luckily he can't hear you now; Eric wouldn't put up with this."

"He'd regret it all the more."

"He'd tear you limb from limb," Roselyn said. "You've no right to task us for our pasts, Athelwynne. Your Master didn't seem well disposed with you. What secret shames do you carry?

"Before Castle Bristlen, I never believed in magic ... except for miracles," Rafe said. "Since then, magic has been our worst foe. First, the Wolflord, then that illusion-giant, then the Valkyrie, and you attack us with walking dead. Now Eloise is cursed! When does it end?"

"Me believe magic," Seren interrupted softly, "but no see evil till Seer. Company not murderers; Seer not join if were. Company like rabbit: Eric lead, chased by Vikings. Seer lead, run from Earl. Seer kill rabbits, no finish quest. Company leave Seer, Eric doomed."

"No!" Eloise shouted, surprising everyone. *"I led them here! I told Eric to lie! It's ... it's my fault!"*

Suddenly Eloise sprang at the Seer and pounded him with her tiny fists. The Seer shoved her off and rose angrily, taller, more dangerous, hands held high as if to blast Eloise from existence.

"No, Eloise ...!" the Seer relaxed, lowering his hands, although his growl never left his voice. "I won't be your suicide-tool. Seren's right; as much as I hate you, I can only go on ... or abandon my Lady's quest." The Seer turned away and faced the ruins of his childhood home. "Give thanks to the Lady; only Her will is sparing you. Just stay out of my way for the rest of our journey."

"Is it still possible?" Roselyn asked. "Can we still go on ... after what's happened?"

"We have to try."

"What of Eloise?" Rafe asked. "The moon will be full again tonight! If we can hide her under a cloak ..."

"That won't help," the Seer sneered. "There are several theories about restraining a werewolf ..."

"Don't call me that!" Eloise cried.

"That's what you are," the Seer said cruelly. "None of my processes would be ... painless, and all will take a lot of work."

"Let's start now, since we don't have much time," Karl said. "Ummmm ..., where do we start?"

"Among the dead," the Seer answered.

Rafe stood sweating before the bright-burning forge with a broken Viking sword in his hands.

"Fire's ready," Rafe said, poking at the glowing coals. "Where're the girls?"

"Still scavenging," Karl said grimly, sitting on a blackened bench with a dagger, carving inlaid silver from the side of a rusty axe head. "I don't understand why gold won't work."

"Gold is the sun's metal," the Seer said, pausing from his hammering to take a breath and re-focus his eyes. "In sunlight, gold shines brightest. Under moonlight, silver shines brightest. For lycanthropes, the moon's predominant when full; that's why they're affected only then, usually including the night before and after. The moon's influence connects them to another plane which transforms them to a darker form of existence, which earthly weapons can't affect. Silver, the moon's metal, fuses them to our reality, and cancels out their lycanthropic immunity."

"We're not trying to kill her," Karl reminded.

"Death is Eloise's only salvation," the Seer said. "A lycanthrope's soul is forfeit; while alive, she's a threat. We aren't the first people trying to keep a lycanthrope confined, but every experiment has utterly failed. I'm helping because I need Eloise, and because chances to study this come rarely. This could work, but it could be fatal. We won't have a choice. Should Eloise break free, we kill her ... or die."

"I know," Karl scowled.

"I won't harm Eloise, no matter what," Rafe said. "Her soul isn't lost: the devil may have it, but God hasn't forsaken her."

"We won't save anyone if the girls don't get back soon," Karl said. "We still have lots to do, and the sun's nearly set. Would you summon them, Seer?"

"If you wish to talk without me ...?"

"I do. Please ...?"

With a scowl, the Seer dropped his hammer and walked out of the burned-out skeleton of his dead father's workshop.

"It's all right, Rafe," Karl said. "If the Seer's plan doesn't work, we'll grab the horses and ride away. Wolves can't run as fast as horses. Once she changes, we needn't worry for her; she's invulnerable."

"Until morning," Rafe mumbled slowly. "If we come back too early, then Eloise'll kill us. If we come too late, then Eloise may kill herself."

"What can we do?"

"Cure her."

"The Seer said there's no cure."

"Not in this world," Rafe said. "As much as I loved Eric, I've never been at ease with this quest, going into an evil land to give Eric's soul to a pagan God, but even the Seer doesn't know what we'll find there. If we have to descend into Hell, maybe we can bring back something useful."

"Find a cure for Eloise beyond the 'crack in the world'?" Karl shrugged.

"Why not?" Rafe asked.

Roselyn, Seren, and Eloise marched in, set down a small pile of weapons and trinkets, and then they turned and left with only dirty looks. The Seer entered as they departed.

"They've been searching through claw-rended Viking corpses," he said. "Ugly task."

"They've never prepared forge, cut inlay, or hammered plate," Rafe said.

"Explain it to them," the Seer said.

The Seer's hammer rung endlessly as he resumed planishing silver scraps into small strips, heating as he went. Karl slowly scraped paper-thin silver inlay out of etched grooves. The amount seemed hardly worth the effort, but as they were doing it for Eloise, not to sell the metal, he grumbled quietly. They'd already melted the Seer's small silver knife and tiny silver buttons from Rafe's vest, but it wasn't enough.

Rafe fumbled through the new items the women had brought; swords, another axe, and daggers all traced with fine silver etchings.

"Look here ...!" Rafe cried. "Buckles! Silver buckles and buttons! Drop those flimsy etchings! These are what we need!"

"Are you sure?" the Seer asked. "They could be plated."

"Not these!" Rafe said. "The girls must have found a rich one! And look at this bosse! Thin, but its back is silver!"

"Get started," the Seer said. "We haven't much time."

While the Seer fanned the flames, Rafe used tongs to set a large buckle in the fire, and Karl scavenged a heavier hammer. When the silver began to grow molten, Rafe dropped the hot buckle atop an anvil and Karl beat it flat until it was a thin wafer; they repeated the process with each silver buckle and button. Then they threw the thin wafers into an iron crucible, where they quickly melted.

The Seer lifted a Viking scramsax, a short, thick sword, with a sharp point and a big crossguard. He dipped its brass pommel, hilt, and crossguard into the molten silver, using a stick to help coat it.

"Don't you want to coat the blade?" Rafe asked.

"A silver blade would kill her," the Seer snapped. "Leave the thinking to me; my thoughts are beyond you."

"Can't prove it by me," Karl retorted.

After lightly coating the pommel, crossguard, and grip with silver, the Seer coated the manacle Rafe had made, a steel bar which Rafe had bent into an 'S', each loop just big enough for one of Eloise's small wrists.

By the time the swordgrip and the manacle were finished, darkness had fallen. The Seer took three daggers with inlay, smeared the last of the molten silver onto their blades, and handed one to Karl, one to Rafe.

"If all else fails ...!"

Rafe complained, yet Karl calmed him; the Seer wouldn't harm Eloise while they lived.

Roselyn walked into the smithy.

"The moon will rise soon," Roselyn said. "I hope you're ready; Eloise's frantic, and Seren and I won't see her hurt anymore."

No one spoke, but all eyes turned to the Seer.

For the first time ever, the Seer looked unsure. He stuck the heavy hammer in his belt, held up his braised, silver-plated dagger, and examined it in the firelight.

"I'm blameless if this doesn't work," he said quietly, almost whispering. "I've done my best. Just make sure our horses are ready, in case we have to ride out fast."

Roselyn carried a crude torch, the scramsax, and the silver manacle while Rafe, the Seer, and Karl strained to carry the heavy iron anvil out to a small wooded area. Roselyn called out, and soon Seren arrived with Eloise, who looked downcast, as if approaching her gallows.

They set the anvil behind a big tree.

"It's time," the Seer said at last, motioning Eloise forward. "I was taught by my masters that, once bitten by a werewolf, the only cure is death. Tonight I'm going to prove them wrong. The Lady hasn't gifted me with all of Her wisdom, but what we're about to do should work ... according to everything that I've learned. If not ..., you'll probably kill us all."

Rafe started to protest but Karl stopped him. Eloise buried her tears against the Seer's robe.

"Wh-what are you going to do?" Eloise asked, her voice timid, breathless.

"Restrain you," the Seer said. "Details are unimportant. Do you want me to try ... or not?"

"What choice do I have ...?"

The Seer glanced down for an uncomfortable moment; Rafe wondered if he actually felt anything for Eloise's misery, but he said nothing.

The Seer took Eloise's hand and led her to the tall tree, where he had her sit and lean back against it. Gently he drew her arms back around its wide trunk. Rafe and Karl came to help. Grunting and straining, and with much hammering, they bent the silver-coated steel bar tight around Eloise's wrists, shackling her to the tree.

"That should hold her," Karl said after trying to bend the bar with all of his might.

"Werewolves has no limits on strength, and my masters have been studying such things since man first walked on this island," the Seer said. "We need to sap her wolf-powers, yet I can only do it as moon rises, and then I must be alone with her."

"Are you going to bind Eloise with magic?" Roselyn asked.

"No power of mine can restrain her," the Seer said. "She's beyond all limits of human wizards."

"Look!" Seren pointed. "Moonrise!"

All eyes turned to east. Through the branches peeked the first pale sliver of the white moon, its crown barely above the horizon. Eloise started to cry.

"We must be alone!" the Seer insisted.

Rafe and Karl exchanged glances. Rafe didn't want to leave Eloise or trust the Seer alone with her, yet he had no choice. Without the Seer, they'd have had to leave Eloise now, perhaps never to see her again, or kill her outright to spare her the pain of her godless curse.

"Be brave, my princess," Rafe kissed Eloise's cheek. "I love you. We'll find a way to save you."

Next, Roselyn knelt and kissed her. "My precious Eloise! Try not to think about what'll happen. Remember what we said. Try to control it, and don't let go. We'll be here in the morning."

Karl came next; the Seer stamped and stared at the rising moon, anxious yet ignored.

"We love you," Karl said. "Hold on, and we'll be right back."

Karl kissed her.

The moon was now half-risen; Seren quickly kissed Eloise on top of her head. "Remember Titania. She protect. Now trust Seer," Seren turned a steely glare upon him. "Only hope."

Quickly Seren walked away, back toward the burned village.

"Take care of her," Karl said to the Seer, and he followed the others. Rafe hurried to catch up with Seren, who pushed him away, crying. Roselyn and Karl were similarly clenched, comforting each other; they could do nothing else. They walked eastwards, toward Grusshire, and stared into the full moon as it rose mercilessly upwards.

Suddenly Eloise screamed, loud and terrible in the dark, silent night. Instantly they turned and ran back.

In the torchlight hovered Eloise, now standing, her arms still shackled around the tree, but her head had fallen to one side. The silver-handled Viking scramsax was stabbed deep through her chest into the trunk behind her. The Seer stood before her, hammer in hand, and he pounded on its pommel, nailing Eloise's corpse to the tree.

Eloise was dead.

Roselyn struck first, knocking the hammer from the Seer's grasp. Karl's fist cracked into the Seer with such force that the Druid fell and rolled head over heels. Seren ran to Eloise's pinned dead body, grabbed the silver-hafted sword, and strained to pull it free from Eloise's corpse. Rafe roared like an angry lion and drew his sword, raising it at the Seer.

"Liar ...! Traitor ...!" Rafe shouted.

"We trusted you ...!" Karl shouted.

"Stand back," Rafe growled at the others. "I'll kill him."

"No ...!" the Seer reeled. *"You don't ...! Leave her alone! Get back! Look out!"*

Eloise's dead eyes popped open. A scream no human could voice retched from her mouth. Though nailed to the tree, and stabbed through the heart, Eloise began to shake. Black, hot smoke poured from her wound with a stench Hell couldn't match. Eloise howled in agony. The soft, light down on her arms grew to long yellow hairs, then to shaggy golden fur. Her face became veiled in curly blonde hair. Teeth swelled from a mouth bent painfully outwards. Nails burst forth long, ripping claws.

"Look out ...!" the Seer cried, and he jumped past Rafe to tackle Seren, who'd clung petrified to the silver hilt, frozen with fear. He hurled her away from Eloise's deadly jaws. Quickly he snatched up the fallen hammer and grabbed the silver swordgrip. Eloise snarled and leaned to bite him, but the Seer hammered once into her face, then onto the pommel three times, driving it harder and deeper into the tree trunk behind her, each time making Eloise howl so loudly leaves fell from nearby trees.

Finally the ghastly stench drove even the Seer back, where he fell exhausted.

Eloise strained, growling and howling to no avail, yet she didn't give up. She threw herself forward to jar the sword from her chest, but as soon as her chest touched its silver hilts, Eloise screamed and was knocked back against the tree.

"Oh, Seer bless you ...!" Roselyn shouted. *"It's working ...!"*

"For the moment," the Seer sneered, wiping the blood from his lip where Karl had punched him, "but how long it'll work, I don't know."

"Poor Eloise ...!" Seren sobbed. *"Lady, no ...!"*

"Forgive me, Seer," Rafe said. "I thought ..."

"Keep your lies to yourself, idiot!" the Seer snapped. "Besides the fact that you don't trust me, your stupidity almost cost Seren's life! I'm a sorcerer! Don't presume to question what I do! It's certainly beyond you!"

"He didn't know ...!" Karl cried.

"How many times are you going to use that excuse?" the Seer demanded. "If I'd told you, would you have stood by and let me run her through? Would any of you have, despite the fact that it had to be done?"

"Athelwynne ...!" Roselyn cried over Eloise's howls. "Stop it! You're the one who insists that we stay together. Why? To help you? Well, you better start earning our help!"

"What more can I do?" the Seer cried. "We're wasting our time experimenting with a werewolf while Eric wanders farther out of reckoning! A light shower could destroy his tracks, and I'll never find him again! But here I am, watching my hopes evaporate. What more do you want of me?"

"Nothing!" Seren said, turning her back on Eloise. "Do everything, but no give, ever!"

"Look out!" Karl cried suddenly, and he pushed Seren down onto the ground.

Straining until the silvered-steel bar could withstand no more, Eloise snapped her steel manacle, snagged Karl's mail-coat, and yanked him into her deadly grip. Impulsively Rafe sprung forward and stabbed his sword between Eloise's slavering jaws as she lunged at Karl's throat, seized Eloise's right arm, and wrenched it free before her savage claws shredded Karl.

The Seer slashed Eloise's left forearm from elbow to wrist with his silver knife. Eloise howled in pain, and as she did, Rafe tore his sword free as Karl fell away.

With a surge, Eloise pushed away from the tree, but as she struck the silvered-hilts, Eloise howled in agony and was knocked back, twisting and biting at the silver-plated swordhilt sticking out her chest.

Roselyn fell onto her knees and sobbed.

Eloise quit stinging herself on the silver grip and glanced about for anything in reach. Quickly she caught up her flimsy dress and shredded it into rags.

Rafe looked pitifully upon her, surprised to see her shape relatively unchanged, more human than wolfish, just covered with a thick coat of blonde fur with a long fall of sun-bright yellow hair hanging behind her.

"You know," Rafe said, "Eloise isn't nearly as inhuman as the Wolflord."

"The Wolflord looked wolfish even before he changed," Karl said.

"This's only Eloise's second transformation," the Seer explained as he wiped his silver blade off on the grass. "The longer she lives, and the more damage she suffers, the worse she'll become. Eventually lycanthropes cease to revert, just become human-ish animals, and finally wild wolves."

"Happen slowly, no ...?" Seren asked.

"Usually," the Seer said. "Unless she should be killed and buried right after a full moon. King Nebuchadnezzar of Babylon was the first to document werewolves ..."

"Shut up ...!" Roselyn screamed. "You talk like she's not even here ...!"

Rafe and Karl exchanged glances, and both held and consoled Roselyn.

"I've done all I can," the Seer said. "Eloise is restrained, for the moment, which means we're alive. Yet Roselyn's right; we should refrain from saying anything we don't want Eloise to know; there's a chance Eloise will remember tonight better than last night."

"Like real wolf ...?" Seren asked. "Farmers make wolves pets, Seren hear. Teach Eloise to no harm ...?"

"Eloise isn't a wolf," the Seer shook his head. "Her curse is older than the Druid race, perhaps older than mankind. Many Druids have sought to cure werewolves, burying them in caves, chaining or caging them in silver. Most start out hopeful, but the longer we hold her, the angrier she'll grow.

"Werewolves grow stronger as they get angrier. The sword pinning her saps her strength, but not enough; I thought she'd be in too much pain to notice us, but she's not. I've little hope this'll keep her pinned."

Eloise began growling, snapping worse than ever, clawing at the swordhilt again and tearing bark off the tree behind her. Seren paled to ashen-white.

"Maybe we should get the horses," Karl suggested.

"The horses are saddled and ready, but the Seer told me not to bring them," Rafe said.

"When Eloise transformed, they would've bolted," the Seer said. "If it looks like Eloise is going to break free, we'll run for it. Karl, you and Rafe could cut off her legs ..."

"That's it ...!" Rafe cried. *"I won't hurt Eloise ...!"*

"You can't hurt her!" the Seer insisted. "We'd be riding out of here before Eloise heals enough to chase us."

"Stop it ...!" Roselyn broke into tears. *"Stop it ...! Just stop ...!"*

"That tears it!" Karl said angrily. "Rafe, Seren, take Roselyn and mount up. We're riding. Seer, come with us. If Eloise is going to break free, I want us long gone when she does. If she doesn't, we'll find out when we come back in the morning."

"We can't," the Seer said. "We have to free Eloise before dawn."

"Free her ...?" Karl asked incredulously.

"What do you think will happen to Eloise when the sun rises, if she reverts back with that sword stuck through her chest?"

No one spoke. Rafe didn't know whether he was shocked or angry; he hadn't thought about that, and obviously none of the others had, either.

"How free Eloise ...?" Seren asked.

"I'd rather not say," the Seer looked down.

"Tell us," Rafe growled.

"Why ...?" the Seer demanded. "You've already condemned me! I'm doing what you ordered, so don't complain about my methods! There are no other methods! Unless any of you can do better, stop blaming me!"

"You're right," Rafe said. "We should've trusted you. But don't blame us. Magic's our bane, and it just gets worse!"

"And worse, beyond the crack in the world, where we're going," the Seer said pointedly. "Magic's often unpleasant; even I get disgusted, but you wanted Eloise held, so I did."

"No more surprises!" Karl snapped with a dirty look. "What are you planning?"

"Just before dawn," the Seer growled, his teeth gritted into a snarl, "we use your steel swords to cut off Eloise's arms and legs. While she's helpless, we pull out the sword and ride away. By the time Eloise heals, we'll be out of town, and we won't turn back until it's full daylight. Eloise won't have gotten far, and she'll be whole again."

Rafe gasped. It seemed cruel, despite that he knew it couldn't harm her.

What kind of monster was the Seer to think up such twisted plans?

Suddenly Eloise howled: a violent, piercing scream. She became frenzied, stomped hairy feet, swung deadly claws, and bared long fangs, her wolf's face twisted with rage. Eloise jumped up, as best she could, and then fell upon the sharp blade; the cut in her chest ripped higher as blood spurted in every direction. Eloise jumped again, and again, and each time she fell, the cut ripped longer, higher, until it seemed she'd slice herself in half.

Black smoke arose, healing as she cut herself more and more.

"Run ...!" the Seer cried. *"Run ...!"*

The companions followed as the Seer dashed for their horses. Only Rafe didn't run; Rafe stood frozen in horrified amazement as Eloise forced the cut in her chest higher and higher until, with a shriek, she tore the sharp blade out of the side of her throat and fell, half-severed, onto the bloodstained ground. Reeking of sulfur, the black smoke burst in a thick cloud, enveloping her.

"Rafe ...!" Karl shouted. *"Run ...!"*

Rafe ran; fast as ever his thick legs pumped for the horses.

Abruptly Seren tripped, screamed, and fell. Rafe caught up to her, and then turned to look back.

Howling furiously, Eloise emerged from the trees.

Seren lay sprawled upon the ground, clutching her ankle. Rafe tried to pick Seren up, but too slowly.

Eloise charged, ready to kill.

"Oh, Lady ...!" Seren cried.

"Go ...!" Rafe cried at Seren, yet she couldn't.

He turned to Eloise and drew his silver-plated knife. He'd sworn not to hurt her, but what choice did he have? Rafe drew back, his deadly dagger tight in his grip and poised to stab, as Eloise charged closer.

"God forgive me ...!" Rafe shouted.

"Titania ...! Help ...!" Seren cried.

Suddenly strange lights burst from the trees, flashing towards Eloise. Eloise jumped and stumbled as the lights dashed between her legs, yet they never touched her. Around and around Eloise the lights spun, swirling in tight, glowing circles. Eloise swatted at them, but they moved too fast.

They looked like large, colorful fireflies, only faster and brighter. Slowly they began to move away, and Eloise chased after them, swatting futily as they danced before her.

Rafe lifted Seren and carried her to the others, inside the only standing barn. As he reached them, the Seer laughed.

"Ha!" the Seer shouted. "I forgot to mention: magic attracts magic!"

"What happened ...?" Rafe asked.

"Titania ...!" the Seer laughed. "Seren called upon her ... and the local fairies responded! They must've been watching us all along! Here I am, a learned magician, and a slut's spell saves us!"

"Don't call her that!" Rafe shouted.

"Stand back," the Seer said. "We can't let the fairies risk their lives."

The Seer stood tall and rigid, suddenly silent and humorless, as dark and unreachable as ever. Eyes closed, his arms raised. Tiny lights danced off his fingertips, growing bigger and brighter as they drifted away.

As they watched, the Seer's lights floated toward Eloise, and then the lights she'd been chasing vanished in a blink, flying off into the dark woods. Eloise turned her attention to the new attraction that the Seer had summoned. The floating lights drifted down the road, and Eloise followed, snarling and futily swatting at them.

The Seer slowly waved his fingers in tiny circles.

"There," the Seer said. "Those illusion-lights will dance around Grusshire all night ... and even a werewolf can't hurt them. Now let's get out of here!"

Chapter 8

Reunion

THE SEER

These murderers killed my father, my friends, and my village ... and my mother's missing.

Silently the Seer cursed as he led them back into the blackened ruins of Grusshire. Again his father would be ashamed of him: his father would've ripped his companions apart with the strength of his blacksmith's arms ... and he'd have expected his son to do no less ... to anyone who'd killed one of their kin.

The Seer bowed his head; he couldn't put personal vengeance above the will of the Lady, but his father would've never understood that.

As long as the Seer could remember, his father had towered over him, more muscles in each arm than the Seer would ever possess, but he was a simple craftsman; the Seer had been born small, subtle, and clever. They'd never understood each other, and when the Seer disdained blacksmithing to become a Druid mage, his father had cast him from the family.

Even in death, the Seer was a disappointment.

Dawn's first rays illuminated a hopeless, dead village. The Seer ordered them to ride behind him, secretly because he loathed the idea of riding beside his father's murderers. He purposely avoided the grim main street; the litter of broken bones that now paved its road were his friends and relations, and he'd rather not ride horses over their memories. He would've liked to clean them all up, to shovel them into the open grave they'd dug, and then he could abandon these killers and search for his mother, but he had a sacred mission to complete.

Eric was getting too far ahead; he could brook no more delays.

Behind the fallen smithy, the Seer summoned his lights, which came mindlessly floating out of the woods. In her wolf-form, Eloise was still attacking the colored lights, angrily snarling and clawing at the intangible specs. Yet, as she emerged into the sunlight, the floating lights vanished, and Eloise screamed. She fell, writhed in agony, and slowly, cruelly transformed back into the little baroness; the Seer watched intently, trying to remember it so he could document it later.

She'd helped murder Grusshire; he should enjoy watching her suffer ... as his father would ... yet he didn't.

Again, the Seer was a disappointment.

The others ran to help and comfort Eloise. The Seer observed their concern with contempt; if he were laying there, suffering, they'd laugh and walk away.

Would he kill them when their quest was finished? Although rare, Druids practiced human sacrifice. Perhaps, when he didn't need these murderers any longer ...

The Seer dismounted and walked up behind them as Karl gently cradled Eloise and the others crowded close around her.

"How do you feel?" the Seer asked Eloise.

The companions glared at him.

"How often does one get to ask such a question?" the Seer insisted, yet no one answered him.

He scowled; this information could be important someday, and what sorcerer wouldn't want to know? He'd read about such curses on the Isle, during his training, yet not once in his lifetime had a lycanthrope been reported.

"We need to get going," the Seer said. "We still have no food or ..."

"There's food in the valley," Rafe said. "Good food, all we can eat; we've friends there."

"Friends you didn't kill ...?"

Glares intensified. The Seer felt bad for being so insensitive, yet he tried not to let it show; they didn't deserve his sympathies.

The companions sat for an hour comforting Eloise while the Seer angrily paced. Karl refused to hurry; the Seer suspected they were purposely infuriating him. He fumed; *how dare these murders tax his patience!* Would they have held their daggers unsheathed if he'd killed Eric? No, they would've slain him outright, no matter what it cost them. The Seer was proud of his restraint; *it proved he was better than they.*

The Seer stomped away, walking through the burned-out ruins of Grusshire. Tears started in his eyes as he recalled the prosperous village he'd grown up in, yet he forced the moisture back; crying was loss of control ... and he couldn't show weakness.

Gone. All of Grusshire, his whole childhood, was lost, taken from him like the Isle had been. His very existence was a string of broken bridges, places he loved, yet couldn't return to. Even his home in Madrone was gone.

How many more homes must he lose ...?

A single tear dripped down his cheek. The Seer brushed it away before anyone saw it, and he forced himself to think of other things.

The Lady; even She seemed to have deserted him, yet he could still feel Her goodness buried deep inside him. Fools called him a blasphemer, but he'd prove them wrong; he wouldn't desert Her, and after he'd proven his loyalty, he'd be vindicated forever, and all his wrongs redressed. The whole Druid Council would bow before him, and he'd own the Isle and the Lady's love.

It was a dream, perhaps, yet it was the only way he wouldn't end up growing old alone.

"Pack Eloise, if you must," the Seer ordered. "We have to leave."

"Shut your mouth!" Karl shouted back at him.

"Tonight's the last night of the full moon," the Seer said to Karl. "Do you want to have time to prepare for Eloise's next transformation ... or not?"

The Seer smirked; he loved asking questions fools couldn't answer.

A few minutes later, they rode out of Grusshire. The Seer was starving; he was accustomed to fasting, but fasting was usually a lazy, peaceful time of mental reflection and spiritual harmony, not hiding in swamps and running from Earls and werewolves.

Arduous fasting ached ...!

Mounted, the Seer led them into the familiar western woods, where he grew up playing. He tried to not look around; the sights and smells of these hills would bring back painful memories, and he couldn't afford tearful reminisces about his childhood haunts while his companions watched.

Occasionally the Seer heard whispering voices; they were scheming against him. Yet he ignored it.

Eloise's curse worked in his favor: if they killed him now, then they'd have to kill Eloise.

But if they turned against him again then he'd hold nothing back! They would suffer the deaths they deserved ...!

Two long hours later, the Seer spotted something new; near the bushes beside the road stood a fresh grave. It was neatly tended, as if it hadn't been there long. A white cross planted at its head read 'Sir Athelred', and several smaller lines described his lineage, crudely carved into the wood after it was painted. The Seer wondered briefly about it, recalled Roselyn saying something about thieves, yet he rode past it without stopping.

By mid-afternoon, they rode out of the foothills. The lowland fields were mostly overgrown, yet they crossed the valley almost to its end. Smoke was pouring from the chimney of the largest farmhouse ... and that meant food.

"Farmer Tiller ...!" Roselyn cried as they rode inside his gates.

A tall, old farmer looked up and waved at them from inside a pen of clucking chickens. A farmwife and a toddler ran out to meet them; Roselyn and Eloise dismounted and hugged them tightly.

"This is Lady Seren and ..., uh, ... Father Athelwynne," Roselyn said amid their greetings.

The Seer nodded politely to the farmer, who bowed in deference to his black robes. The Seer was trepidatious; he wondered how they'd explain Eloise's condition.

"Pleased to meet you," Farmer Tiller said to the Seer with a queer look. "But where's Eric? I wouldn't expect him to lag behind."

"Forgive us," Karl said, bowing his head. "I fear ... we bring bad news."

"I'd better sit down for this," Farmer Tiller said grimly. "Let's go inside."

Their house was large and comfortable, rustic, not as grand or austere as the Seer's house in Madrone, yet his wife brought them cool beer and fresh, small loaves with lots of honey-butter. They ate every loaf so quickly she jokingly scolded them, and then hurried into the kitchen to prepare an early supper.

Farmer Tiller's young sons soon arrived from the fields. Karl told Farmer Tiller their whole story, with the others constantly interrupting. The Seer felt concerned about trusting this peasant, yet saw no point in complaining; the farmer asked many sly questions, and the Seer suspected he learned a great deal more than Karl said in words.

Karl tried his best to shy around the Seer's part, but Farmer Tiller waved him on.

"Don't hide one apple when you're showing me the bushel," Farmer Tiller laughed. "If 'Father Athelwynne', or whatever your real name is, is a

Christian priest, then I'm a rabbit; I recognize a Speaker of the Lady when he enters my house."

"Most folk call me Seer," he hesitantly offered his hand.

"We're honored," Farmer Tiller said, shaking hands. "Perhaps you'll be around to join us for the Summer Circle?"

"If I am, I certainly shall."

"I didn't know you worshiped the Lady!" Rafe said to the farmer.

"Always have," Farmer Tiller grinned. "Royalty and folk trying to impress them may have converted to the new God, but most farmers around here still follow our family's traditions. The Lady's taken care of us for generations."

Karl told Farmer Tiller everything, including their misadventures before arriving at his door a month ago under dark rainy skies. Farmer Tiller hung on every word and asked many questions, yet he remained mostly silent and listened until Karl was done. Then he sadly reached behind his chair, brought out a large jug, and drank deeply.

"A mighty tale," Farmer Tiller said, passing the jug to Eloise. "If Master Seer weren't here then I'd be inclined to disbelieve it. Poor Eloise! Young lady, if there's anything I can do, my farm is yours."

"That's good," Karl said as Eloise drank from Tiller's jug, "because we lost our treasure to Earl Sir Guldwin and can't pay."

"Eric was your greatest treasure," Farmer Tiller said sadly. "Don't worry; the pieces of treasure you gave us will pay for the rest of your lives."

"Pieces ...?" Karl asked. "Eric gave you coins."

"I gave Mrs. Tiller a gold bracelet," Roselyn confessed.

"I gave her a silver ring box," Rafe laughed.

"I gave her sons jeweled daggers," Eloise said, and both Nate and Phil stood and proudly displayed the prizes strapped to their belts.

"Eric gave us something else," Farmer Tiller said, "his silver knife and mead-flask. I was to offer them to the Vikings, if they found us, as a token that Eric was here. He said Svenson might suffer us to live if he were appeased."

Everyone smiled except the Seer.

"I hate to break this mood," the Seer said, "but the afternoon's passing swiftly. Tonight will be the last full moon of this month and Eloise will ... change. We must take care that none of your family's endangered."

"Yes, that's true," Farmer Tiller nodded, "I'd like to help, if I can."

"And me!" shouted Nate.

"Me, too!" echoed Phil.

"Boys, go help your mother in the kitchen ... *Now!"* Farmer Tiller ordered. The boys tried to argue, but their father shouted and they scurried off, whining. "Sorry," he said. "Now, what are you planning, and how can I help?"

"I plan to hinder her by restricting her attacks to false images," the Seer said. "They'll harmlessly wander your fields from moonrise to dawn, drawing her attention, and keep her from running off. All I need is a field far enough apart that no house can be seen from it. With your family and my .., uh, companions ... boarded inside, it should be safe."

"What about you?" Farmer Tiller asked.

"I need be outside only until Eloise has changed," the Seer said. "Then I'll come back."

"I want to go," Rafe said, waving the Seer down as he started to object. "No, Seer, not because I don't trust you; you may need me for protection. Without you, we've no hope of finding a cure for Eloise."

The Seer glared, but nodded assent.

"Farmer Tiller, you amazed me," Roselyn said. "All we've told you is so ... bizarre. Two months ago I wouldn't have believed a word of it, yet you're taking it in stride ... as if you already knew it."

"The Wolflord legend was here when my family first moved into this valley," Tiller said pointedly. "No one ever goes into Wolven Forest, nor has for years. I'm heartened to hear he's dead; now I can claim the lands around Wolven, since nobody wants 'em. It'll be safe now that there's no werewolf around."

Eloise choked, looked down, and took another swig from Tiller's jug.

"Now, little miss," Farmer Tiller scolded, "I didn't mean you. After all, aren't you the new Baroness of Castle Bristlen? You own all these lands, my farm included. Don't fret! You've a Speaker of the Lady with you; She'll help you find a way, and if not, you'll always be welcome here."

"But I'm a ... werewolf."

"A wolf is a noble animal," Farmer Tiller smiled. "You're their queen now, ruling over them as you rule us. Trust the Lady, Eloise. Don't call yourself a werewolf. Call yourself a ... Wolfqueen. That's a good name for a princess like you."

"... Wolfqueen ..?" Eloise repeated, and she swigged hard. "Is that my future? To live in a cave and haunt dark forests that everyone avoids ...?"

"There've been others," the Seer said, "kings and queens with similar afflictions who ruled great empires in the east. They lived in mighty castles filled with great people."

"That's not your future," Rafe said. "We'll find a cure for you, if God allows it."

"And if He doesn't ...?" Eloise asked.

"We'll take care of you," Rafe promised, and everyone chorused agreement, even Farmer Tiller. The Seer said nothing, thinking them fools, but he wished someone cared about him that much.

Sarah, Farmer Tiller's wife, came in.

"Michael, dinner's ready," she smiled. "If everyone's hungry, the table is waiting. This time we have plenty, I'm afraid."

"Unlike our last visit, when Farmer Tiller charged me every silver coin I had for a dry tunic?" Karl asked, and everyone laughed.

"We'll finish this talk later," Farmer Tiller said, and he got up.

Dinner was the same only better. Rafe said a solemn grace, praying for mercy on Eric's soul, thanking God for giving them friends as worthy as the Tillers, and begging for His help with Eloise. Then steaming platters and bowls devoured their attention. Nate and Phil talked ceaselessly on every subject they knew, which the companions politely listened to while they ate. Edith smiled a lot, but mostly she listened to her brothers' chatter and stared at Roselyn, laughing each time Roselyn winked at her.

After dinner, the Seer asked for a place where he could rest. Farmer Tiller obliged, and the Seer followed him to a small room with a shaded window and a large bed. The farmer bowed slightly and promised to keep his boys quiet.

"This Wolflord ...?" the Seer inquired, "Your family ...?"

Farmer Tiller's eyes widened.

"My grandfather," Tiller confessed in a whisper. "Great-grandfather, actually. Only Sarah and I know."

"But Eloise might know ... someday?" the Seer guessed.

"Why not?" Farmer Tiller asked. "Grandfather was a good man. He worked hard and always looked young. He built this house and made fields out of pastureland; you've never met a more-honest man. But he had to 'go visiting' once a month."

"Leave during nights of the full moon," the Seer interpreted, "but he stopped coming home."

"It was his decision," Farmer Tiller said. "He slowly became violent, and started to snarl and hiss. Sometimes he'd sit by the tinderbox for hours, breaking up each little stick into splinters. So he moved out, coming back to visit rarely, so long ago the boys barely remember him. Finally he just stopped coming, but that was after three generations of good living, never aging past forty. I'm glad your friends ended his misery; they helped him, really."

"So, you're thinking Eloise would make a good daughter-in-law, even cursed?" the Seer asked.

"My great-grandmother never complained, and my boys are growing fast," Farmer Tiller said. "There aren't many decent young girls left around here, and Eloise is my baroness. It'd be her choice. Upon the Lady, I swear she'll be well-treated."

"The Lady helps those who call upon Her," the Seer said. "Thanks for your offer, but you should withhold it until we return, if ever."

"Don't go, Speaker," Farmer Tiller pleaded. "I know Vikings. Some have honor, but they can be cruel and brutal, and their Gods are even worse. This 'crack in the world' can only lead to suffering. What could be there that's worth risking your souls?"

"To keep your secret," the Seer ignored his question, "best act more surprised on occult matters. I didn't need the Lady to see through your tale, and my companions are quick-witted."

"I will," Tiller said respectfully, and he bowed deeply. "Thank you, your Grace, and goodnight."

Chapter 9

Surprises

ROSELYN

Evelyn giggled as Roselyn tickled her tummy; Roselyn couldn't remember smiling so widely or having so much fun. Sarah Tiller's daughter was delightful, and Roselyn wondered, hopefully, if she'd ever have a daughter like her. Not wearing her father's armor, she felt curiously light, although conspicuous, still wearing pants and a quilted gambeson like a man. Yet these clothes were warm and soft, and since no one else seemed to notice, she didn't worry about it.

Strangely, Roselyn missed the weight of her armor; it had felt comfortable after she got used to it.

She liked its feeling of strength and invulnerability, and its padded thickness kept her warm even at night.

As the sunlight dimmed outside, Sarah lit candles and sat by her husband before their warm, glowing fireplace. Nate and Phil had been hushed, so little was said. Eloise lay sprawled upon a huge chair gulping from Farmer Tiller's jug as she had since dinner. Karl sat beside her on the arm of her chair.

"Eloise, you may want to go easy on that," Karl said. "It's a powerful brew."

"Sssoooo ...?" she slurred.

"Perhaps it'll do her good," Farmer Tiller said. "It's an old family recipe."

"It'll do good," Sarah said. "It contains special spices; Eloise will regret it in the morning, but that'll pass."

"M-m-maybeee," Eloise stammered, swaying her head. "But I-I ... l-l-like it nowww."

"Relax, princess," Rafe smiled. "Remember, tonight will be your last."

"Let us pray so," Sarah said. "Poor child!"

"No need to fear," Karl reminded everyone. "The Seer says he can control it this time."

"L-like ..(hic) .. like last n-n-n-nigh-t?"

"Eloise, you're drunk!" Roselyn teasingly scolded. "Shame on you! What a sight you'd be at royal court!"

"Itsss okayyyy," Eloise giggled. "I c-can't seeeee!"

They all laughed except Seren, who'd fallen asleep on Rafe's shoulder, cuddled before the warm fire.

Suddenly the Seer entered the room, pale and rigid, his expression void of all emotion.

"It's time," the Seer said, his voice strangely deadened. "Rafe, bring Eloise."

"I want to go," Roselyn said.

"And I," Karl said.

"As you wish," the Seer said in monotone, absently.

"I'd like to go along, too," Farmer Tiller said, and the Seer turned and looked at him.

"It could be ... unpleasant."

"I'll risk it."

"Me, too!" shouted Nate and Phil at the same moment.

"No," Sarah said loudly. "You'll both stay with me and guard Evelyn."

Both boys fussed, but Farmer Tiller paid them no heed, and led the companions out. Karl carried Eloise, who was drunkenly sobbing, unable to walk. Seren stayed behind, still asleep.

"Nnnooo, nooo! Dooonn' make meee g-go ...!" Eloise whined, but they had no choice.

After Rafe was in the saddle, Karl lifted Eloise up to him. Farmer Tiller borrowed Eloise's horse, as she was too crocked to ride, and quickly led them behind his house and down a wide path. Farmer Tiller handled Eloise's horse with experienced ease, and they trotted swiftly north under bright stars. No one spoke, especially the Seer, who seemed distant and never looked directly at anyone. Even when they stopped, at the edge a shadowy pine forest near a crumbling wooden fence, the Seer never lost his glazed look.

"Here's the best place that I can think of," Tiller said.

"It'll do," the Seer said vacantly, his voice raising the hackles on Roselyn's neck. "Rafe, before the moon rises, leave Eloise over by that fence."

"Nnnnoooooo ...!" Eloise slurred, crying.

"Best do it now," Farmer Tiller said. "Here she comes!"

The eastern horizon over the hills of Wolven Forest glowed with the first tip of the white moon. Rafe spurred forward, then carried Eloise down and set her gently by the fence. Rafe kissed her forehead, and then rode back. Roselyn could barely see Eloise in the distance, though the night was clear.

The moon rises fast when full. They waited silently, mounted behind the Seer, who'd dismounted and walked a few steps forward. Plaintively Eloise cried out. Roselyn yearned to help; Eloise had drunkenly staggered upright and stood clinging to the fence to keep from falling, pathetic and alone, sobbing as the heartless moon rose bright and full.

Roselyn caught soft sounds of a mumbled chant, slowly becoming louder and stronger as the moon's light grew. All stared, transfixed on Eloise, helpless to keep the moon from rising or her curse from being real.

The Seer's voice grew powerful, boomed in a language seeming arranged more of sounds than words. The Seer shouted his chant louder as the moon rose full.

Eloise screamed, a final, mortal shriek, and then she fell against the fence, bent over its rail. In the moonlight, her body underwent the same change as before, but this time it happened quicker. Even at their distance, they couldn't miss the sudden rupture of claws and fur. Roselyn burst into tears and Rafe crossed himself.

"I ... n-n-never knew ...," Farmer Tiller stuttered, shocked yet transfixed.

The Seer shouted his echoing chant, and then screamed horribly, a throat-wrenching cry.

From spots all around them, white smoke seeped up out of the ground, faintly glowing, spooky in the sudden silence. Six feet the white puffs wafted, and then they solidified. The smoke coalesced into living human shapes, soft and translucent in the moonlight, white as fresh snow on a deep winter's night. Shapes of men and women formed, sharply defined. Some were dressed as farm peasants, others as warriors from long ago, painted or tattooed with twisting snakes, and some were shaggy, naked in the moonlight, or garbed in loincloth alone. Ghostly faces looked sad and mournful. As one, they gazed at the Seer, and then all turned and began walking slowly away.

"Ghosts ...!" Farmer Tiller cried.

At Farmer Tiller's shout, Eloise whirled, snarling. The Wolfqueen's red eyes fastened on them, glancing at the white figures only briefly. Terror clutched Roselyn; they'd stayed too long. The Wolfqueen probably remembered them torturing her last night, and wanted bloody revenge. Roselyn glanced behind, wondering if they could escape without leading Eloise back to Farmer Tiller's house, too near to Seren, Sarah, and her children.

If they could escape ...!

Eloise threw back her wolf-head and howled.

But her howl sounded squelched, slurred and broken. Eloise pushed herself away from the fence, wobbled, raised a long-clawed hand, and fell flat onto her face.

Only ghostly figures moved, pacing dejectedly around the field and woods beyond, aimlessly wandering in circles. Eloise, the Wolfqueen, lay drunk, out cold.

The Seer stared disbelieving, glanced at Farmer Tiller, and then back at Eloise.

"I must have that recipe!" the Seer exclaimed.

"Me, too," Rafe chuckled, staring at Eloise's blonde wolf-form, drunkenly passed out on the ground.

"B-But ...!" Tiller stammered.

"I warned you ... it'd be unpleasant," the Seer sighed, seeming wearied after his spell-casting. "These are phantoms ... of all who've perished here. But perhaps it was a waste; Eloise seems ... not to need them. What was in that liquor?"

"It was my grandfather's special favorite," Farmer Tiller said slowly. "You're welcome to the recipe; it's no secret, but I never suspected ..."

"We should ride back," the Seer said, clinging weakly to his saddle. "These poor souls will wander harmlessly, but Eloise might wake up."

"We can't just leave her ...!" Roselyn argued.

"What can harm her ...?" the Seer asked.

They rode back together.

Rafe and Karl tried to comfort Roselyn, yet she felt uneasy. Roselyn stayed up late, once riding out with Farmer Tiller and the Seer to check on Eloise; from a distance they saw that Eloise had awakened, but only to wander a few paces before passing out again. When they returned, Roselyn curled up in a big chair before the fire, determined to stay awake all night.

Roselyn awoke to glad scents of frying bacon and spiced tea. Eloise was trying to help Sarah Tiller in the kitchen, yet she was mostly standing aside, struggling to understand the experienced cook's routine. Roselyn smiled; neither she nor Eloise knew much about motherly duties.

Eloise was wearing another peasant blouse and skirt, this time with a brown apron. With the last of the full moons, Eloise's terrible transformations were finished. They'd have a month to prepare for the next one.

Breakfast was a delight, except for Eloise, who regretted her excessive drinking binge after her first bite. At the Seer's suggestion, Sarah brewed a special tea to soothe her pains, made of herbs gleaned from Farmer Tiller's liquor recipe. Roselyn watched them carefully; apparently the Seer and Farmer Tiller had been awake and talking all night, and strange looks glanced between them.

"What you been talking 'bout?" Seren asked.

"This and that," Farmer Tiller said evasively. "The Seer's given me a list of provisions you need. I'd like to help, and maybe you'll visit again when you return. I can't go, of course, but I'd love to hear what happens."

"I'll return, if I'm able," Roselyn said, and everyone agreed.

"Good," Tiller said. "Now, the Seer says you must be off at once ..."

"Yes ...!" the Seer firmly interjected before Roselyn could object. "Eric's been moving for three nights and days, and we've hardly seen any trace of him. We may be riding while Eric's only walking, but he can travel anywhere, and we mustn't be far behind."

"Right," Tiller said, "so after breakfast, we'll go downstairs."

Warmed by a hot meal, all Roselyn wanted to do was laze about, but she followed as Farmer Tiller led them through a false door in the back of a closet to a storeroom filled with kegs, barrels of grain, dried vegetables, and other foodstuffs. Tiller moved a large basket and opened a trapdoor hidden beneath it. Down a steep stairway, they descended into a huge basement filled with all manner of things, some layered with dust untouched for generations. Gamehooks, old saws, long antlers, and wooden chests lined each wall, piled in layers of forgotten junk.

"They're down here somewhere," Farmer Tiller laughed, and he dug in to the clutter. Roselyn offered to help, yet she didn't know what to look for, let alone where to begin.

"Ah, here they are!" Farmer Tiller said, wheezing amid a cloud of dust, and he raised up an old leather bag with handles.

"What's it for?" Rafe asked, coughing.

"It's a backpack, in the old style," Tiller said, and he tossed it to Rafe, who caught the musty bag in a shower of dust. "You loop it on your shoulders and buckle the strap across your chest. The bag hangs down your back. It wears well overtop mail, if you like. They're not as new as the ones I gave you last time, but highly functional."

"It stink!" Seren winced.

"We can fix that," Farmer Tiller said, tossing one to each of the men. "Now wait a second. There're a few other things hidden around here."

If there was something not in Farmer Tiller's basement, they couldn't name it. Climbing upstairs, they found themselves laden with packs, ropes, lanterns, candles, a sextant and compass, heavy cloaks and gloves, and several pairs of old boots and spurs, all coated with a thick layer of dust, causing much coughing and sneezing. But Farmer Tiller carried up many rags and a jug of natural oil; soon everything looked newer, or at least, polished. Even their packs, dried and cracked leather, now gleamed light brown, and the boots he gave Roselyn felt surprisingly soft.

All too soon they stood ready to go. Sarah stuffed four of the packs with dried provisions while Eloise and Roselyn rolled their new cloaks into two bundles to be slung over a horse, and the rest they pocketed best as they could.

Goodbyes were long and sad. Farmer Tiller hugged Eloise and kissed her cheeks, and Sarah hugged them all with kind, motherly warnings, even the Seer, who seemed extremely discomforted in her maternal embrace. Nearing noon, they rode off, although Roselyn's heart stayed behind.

Joking and singing, they laughed as they rode back toward Castle Bristlen, using the main road, skirting Wolven Forest. In greater detail, Rafe told Seren of their adventure in those woods and of his slaying of the Wolflord. Even Eloise spoke a little, which made

Roselyn hope she was getting over her ugliest experience.

"You were lucky," the Seer said. "If not for this Liz Apple, you'd never have slain the Wolflord. Quite a coincidence, having an Isle-trained priestess arrived just in time to save you from a wolf pack; I suspect the Lady was watching over you."

"God helped us both times," Rafe insisted, frowning at the Seer. "I thought we were doomed until He made me remember the silver."

"It could've been the Lady," Karl said.

Rafe rolled his eyes, shook his head, and made the sign of the cross.

"Karl ...!" Roselyn laughed. "You sound like Athelwynne!"

"Her folk saved us from Eloi.., I mean, the Wolfqueen, in Grusshire," Karl reminded them, his hand brushing the golden ribbon Titania had given him. "The fairies must've been watching us then ... as they may be doing now."

"No fairie would inhabit a lycanthrope's lair," the Seer said. "Alas that this Wolflord was a foe no priestess could defeat!"

Eloise bowed her head and said nothing.

The Seer urged them on, especially as the sun set bloody red behind the trees. Rafe led them up a narrow trail he knew well, which saved them from having to ride down towards Demril, and then climb the winding trail up Othar.

In the sun's last rays, they sighted Castle Bristlen, majestically towering like a lonely sentinel over the mighty Atlantic. The last time they'd seen it, bright flames pouring out of windows showed Vikings slaying Saxons on stony battlements, but no more. All was silent and barren. Forbidding Bristlen seemed as the fading light of day eclipsed it, the sky draped by rolling black clouds. No lights shined from battlement, tower, or window; an ominous feeling clenched Roselyn's spine.

Darkness fell fast in the wooded dells as they rode toward Bristlen. Then, in the shadows of early night, the Seer cried out.

"Look ...!" the Seer said joyously, holding his moonstone out over glowing tracks. "Eric! We're back on his trail!"

"We knew that," Karl sneered.

"Really ...?" the Seer asked sarcastically.

"Yes," Karl answered smartly. "Eric's been back-tracking our trail since he died. Of course he came here."

"Eric never walked back through Madrone, or to the hilltop where Skaldi attacked us, so he isn't going everywhere," the Seer said, "Even if he had, how will we follow Eric before he met you? How far back will he go? Demril ...? Norway ...? Will Eric keep following every footstep he ever made, all the way back to his birth?"

"Tell us, if you know," Rafe said.

"Yes," Roselyn said, "and how much longer is this going to take?"

"I don't know," the Seer said. "If I did, I wouldn't have to follow Eric, I'd just lead us there. Eric could leave this course any time he wanted and take off for Valhalla in any direction, and we'd lose his trail forever. Not only would I never get through the 'crack in the world', but Eric would never get into Valhalla."

"I thought you were joking about that," Karl said.

"Me ...? Joke ...?" the Seer looked indignant.

The Seer shook his head and spurred, holding out his moonstone to light Eric's tracks. The companions followed, riding dangerously fast in the darkness, unnerved as the glowing prints vanished under their hooves.

Finally they came to the edge of the forest and looked across a wide grassy field to the stone walls of Castle Bristlen. The towering crenellations seemed higher than when Roselyn had last seen them, and their lack of guards seemed more threatening than a Viking garrison. Yet Eric's bright trail led straight toward the main gate.

"This isn't right," Rafe said. "Vikings held Bristlen; if Earl Guldwin had marched his men here, then Guldwin's men would be manning those walls. One or the other should be here; no one deserts a castle."

They rode to the front gate, following Eric's yellow prints, which glowed atop grass, rocks, and dirt. Roselyn feared they might be seen; they needed the Seer's magic to follow Eric, yet Roselyn didn't want to be seen following ghostly, glowing tracks. Vikings would think them harbingers of evil ... and Christians burned witches.

The broken main gate was braced open by stout poles, yet no one guarded it. No lights or sounds came from within.

"Looks like nobody's home," Karl said.

"Eric's tracks end here," the Seer observed. "They must've been trampled; someone was here when Eric arrived."

"Either way, we have to rest the horses," Rafe said. "Tie them up inside the gate; I need to check the stables before I stall them."

Roselyn glanced inside the empty courtyard, smothered in shadow.

"Who goes first ...?" Roselyn asked.

"Go ahead, Seer," Rafe urged. "This is your specialty."

"All right," the Seer fussed, "but stay close!"

Under the splintered remains of the once-mighty portcullis, they entered Castle Bristlen, their horses' hoof-steps echoing from the courtyard's black shadows. A fierce stench assaulted them; the whole castle reeked of decaying blood, so foul Roselyn strained to hold her breath, reluctant to breathe the awful air. Littered on the ground lay broken arrows and bits of armor; no troops had practiced here since the day before they'd fled. Nervously they dismounted, and tied their horses to posts.

Stumbling through darkness, the Seer held his moonstone high as he led their way across the dim, starlit courtyard. Only axe-cloven boards hanging on scarred hinges remained of the once-sturdy doors to the castle keep. Inside was pitch black, until the Seer's moonstone shone through the doorway, brightly illuminating the great hall with hundreds of glowing 'V's. Roselyn gasped and Rafe crossed himself.

Led by the Seer, hesitantly they entered and crossed the familiar room to the empty thrones, now hacked and battle-scarred. Eric's glowing prints mysteriously vanished as they tread over them.

"Why many glow-marks?" Seren asked.

"I don't know," the Seer whispered.

Suddenly, by the open doorway leading to the Baron's private quarters, a new glowing 'V' appeared, followed by another, closer to them. Roselyn's eyes opened wide, hackles on her neck rising in alarm.

Another glowing 'V' appeared, and then another.

A ghastly phantom materialized out of nowhere. Eric flashed into view, awful and appalling, howling an unearthly, echoing shriek, one morbid arm waving, the other ending in a bloody stump, his expression a twisted mockery of Eric's once-jovial face.

Screaming, all fled, the Seer the out the door first. Roselyn would've run all the way to Demril had the Seer not stopped them in the courtyard.

"Wait ...!" the Seer shouted. "Hold up! We're safe now!"

"That was Eric ...!" Rafe cried, and everyone started shouting.

"Quiet ...!" the Seer shouted. "Eric wouldn't hurt any of you!"

"Then why did you run?" Roselyn demanded.

"If Eric was going to hurt anyone, it'd be me," the Seer said. "But we can't run now. Someone's got to face Eric ...!"

A silence fell. The Seer was right: Eric was their friend. Roselyn tried to summon her courage, yet she trembled.

"I will," Karl said, though his voice cracked. "Eric won't hurt me; I'll go."

"You don't need to go," the Seer warned, his eyes bulging. "Here he comes!"

Yellow 'V's came out the doorway, down the steps, then across the dark, dirt courtyard. Roselyn's terror rose. She and Eloise pushed Karl forward.

"Call him ...!" the Seer cried. "Now, before he gets closer!"

"Eric ...!" Karl cried. *"Eric, it's us! It's Karl, Roselyn and Eloise! We're your friends! Stay back!"*

Eric materialized again, gruesome in the moonlight. Eric hovered translucent before them, his spooky countenance ravaged by a frightful, tormented look, creased by an endless, bitter doom of hopeless wandering. Slowly he gestured to his severed stump, glaring in despair. Seren fainted, yet the rest of them hardly noticed.

"Eric, don't be sad!" Eloise shouted. *"We're here! We're going to help you ...!"*

"The Seer's with us!" Roselyn said. "We've seen the Fairie Queen, and she'll help us, too."

Eric shook his head and slowly turned away.

"We have your arm ...!" the Seer shouted. *"Eric, we're going with you ...! We can still get you into Valhalla ...!"*

At the word 'Valhalla', Eric hesitated. His wispy body seeming to waver, and then grow brighter. Slowly Eric turned back to face them.

"It's true ...!" Karl shouted. "I spoke to the Valkyrie on the battlefield! She said there's still a chance, but only we could do it!"

"Just keep walking!" the Seer instructed. "We can follow your tracks! As long as you lead us on a trail we can follow, we can save you! Use your instincts! Feel for Valhalla! Find a path we can follow!"

"But not tonight!" Roselyn shouted. "We need rest. Meet us tomorrow at dusk, here in the courtyard. We'll stay close by from now on."

"No ...!" the Seer argued. "We'll be hanged if we're seen walking through Demril with you. Meet us in Demril, Eric. Tomorrow night, at dusk, at the docks!"

"Eric ...!" Eloise said, and she hesitantly walked to stand before him, letting her cloak fall to the ground behind her. "Please, Eric, we want to do this. We love you."

Eric held his place, motionless. Roselyn couldn't help wonder what agonies he was suffering, if he heard or understood at all. She doubted if even the Seer had ever experienced anything like this, horrified, poised on the brink of terror, facing a dead man they once called friend. Roselyn didn't know what to say or do. She couldn't reach for Eric; if she did, she couldn't hold him; if she tried, she couldn't comfort him.

Eric's one hand clenched into a fist, and deathly slow, he raised it across his chest in somber salute. Then his spirit grew dim and faded away.

No one moved or spoke for a long, long time.

The stone castle keep was the only building not consumed by fire. They made themselves at home in the late baron's bedroom, after helping Rafe secure their horses in the great hall, since Rafe's old, familiar stable had burned to the ground. Every room in Bristlen had been ransacked, yet the Baron's bedroom still had furniture, wood by the fireplace, and was mostly clean. Quickly they entered, closed the door, and dropped their packs and armor, weary from their unearthly encounter.

Conscious again, Seren stretched out on the baron's bed. The Seer wanted to lay enchantments on the door to keep Eric out, yet the others refused. Around a divan, the Seer drew a circle of salt to protect himself. Smiling, Roselyn got Karl and Rafe to help her with a heavier chore. Returning only minutes after they'd left, Rafe and Karl stumbled into the bedroom carrying the baronial throne.

"Here," Roselyn said, gesturing to the throne. "For you, Eloise."

"N-No ...," she stammered.

"It's yours by right, Baroness," Roselyn said firmly, and she took Eloise by her hand and led her to the throne, whispering secretly in her ear; Eloise brightened and hugged Roselyn. Then, assuming the air of dignity she could at will, Eloise haughtily sat upon the throne of Castle Bristlen, the rightful heir, successor, and lawful ruler of the Barony du Harmonn.

"Let all those present now bear witness," Roselyn sang out, rising tall, and taking her place beside Eloise. "Here now is your lawful ruler, in legal claim of her rightful office, Lordship of the Barony du Harmonn, with all the hereditary rights and responsibilities granted by royal decree. I give you Baroness Eloise Elizabeth du Harmonn. Long live Baroness Eloise!"

"Long live Baroness Eloise ...!" Karl and Rafe gladly shouted.

Eloise smiled wickedly, elated at last.

"Karl, Rafe, and Athelwynne, come forward and kneel before your baroness," Roselyn ordered.

The men hesitated, suddenly confused. The Seer had been only absently watching, as if they were children playing a game.

Rafe shrugged and knelt before Eloise. Grudgingly Karl joined him. Both turned and stared at the Seer, who'd joined Seren, sitting on the bed.

Grunting his disgust, the Seer rose and, softly cursing, joined them on his knees. Grinning devilishly, Eloise stood and nodded to Roselyn. Roselyn smiled and spoke out in a crisp, clear voice.

"Karl, Rafe, and Athelwynne, by the power vested by royal decree to the Baronial Sovereign of du Harmonn, mindful of your service to her and her barony, and after consultation with her loyal subjects, her Excellency Baroness Eloise is minded to bestow upon you the rightful ennoblement of the order of knighthood. Do you accept?"

"You're jesting," Karl said.

"Not at all," Roselyn said. "The power to create knights comes with the hereditary office of Baron, written in specific clauses and signed by the king."

"And exactly what 'loyal subjects' have you discussed this with ...?" the Seer asked. "Roselyn ...?"

"Countess Roselyn," Eloise reminded them. "Seren, do you think these worthy men deserve knighthood?"

"Yes ...!" Seren laughed.

"I accept," Rafe said, flashing a smile at Seren.

"You can't be serious!" Karl argued. "Knights have to come from noble families, be trained, and have studied! I'm just a ..."

"My father knighted men for everything from luck in a tournament to getting the right girl pregnant," Roselyn said. "Most were squires, but as many were for politics as bravery. Anyone who holds the authority to confer knighthood may decide their own qualifications, as Eloise has done."

"Why would I want to be a knight?" the Seer asked. "I don't fight with swords or wear metal, and my studies haven't been aimed at military campaigns. I'm sorry, Baroness, but I can't accept."

"Think," Roselyn said to the Seer. "Knights don't pay taxes, and have many special rights, but it's your choice. Eloise would at least like for you to swear to her as an advisor."

"So that's what you want ...!" the Seer snapped. "Oath of fealty; our pledges to obey your commands, which would make you our leader!"

"I am your leader, Druid," Eloise said, leaning forward with frown. "You, too, live under the laws of this land, to which I was born successor ... Baroness of du Harmonn!"

"A successor the Earl of Northumbria has put a bounty upon," the Seer reminded her. "The king may undo anything you dare."

"That's not yours to decide," Roselyn said. "Much will be debated before anything serious happens, and until then, the king's word is law: Eloise is Baroness."

No sword could cut the sudden silence as the Seer turned his contemptuous stare on Eloise, who returned it angrily, ready for a fight.

"Yes," Karl said, "but Eloise will always be my princess. Sorry, Seer, but I never expected to make Watchmaster. I can't pass this up, and no oath of fealty could make me do more for Eloise than I already would. Yes, Baroness Eloise; I accept."

"Consider, Seer," Eloise said. "Knighthood grants benefits you can't otherwise achieve."

"Not to mention obligations: to fight in wars ... and stay on a royal leash, which I'm not prepared to accept. Thank you, but the Lady provides all I need. Besides; what mortal vow could supersede my oath to Her?"

"As you wish," Roselyn said. "Seer, you have Eloise's permission to withdraw."

The Seer got up and sat back on the bed; he'd won, but he still frowned.

"Draw your swords," Roselyn said solemnly to Karl and Rafe, "and hold them up, before you in both hands."

Karl and Rafe did so, and Eloise reached down and put one hand on each of their blades.

"Repeat after me," Roselyn said. "Upon my honor, and by the grace of God, St. George, and St. Michael, I do hereby swear fealty and service to

Baroness Eloise Elizabeth du Harmonn and the Kingdom of England, swearing my life and soul to the cause of chivalry, to come and to go, to do and to let be, to strike and to spare, to speak and to be silent, to be true and just in all matters, forever courteous, in war or peace, in famine or plenty, in sickness or health, in living or dying, until I am released from my vows, death take me, or the world end. So say I, Karl of du Harmonn and Rafe of du Harmonn."

"And this do I swear to reward," Eloise said seriously after they'd repeated Roselyn's oath, "loyalty with protection, valor with honor, and oathbreaking with vengeance. And now, by the power vested in me as rightful sovereign of the Barony du Harmonn, and by the grace of St. George and St. Michael ..."

Eloise lifted Karl's sword from his hands, held it above him, and brought down its tip to touch gently on his right shoulder, then his left, and then his head.

"... I hearby dubb thee Knight. Arise, Sir Karl of du Harmonn," she said, then she sheathed his sword in its scabbard on his belt, took Rafe's sword, and repeated her motions.

"By the grace of St. George and St. Michael, I hearby dubb thee Knight. Arise, Sir Rafe of du Harmonn, and the blessings of God upon you both!"

Eloise hugged them both as Roselyn and Seren cheered.

Suddenly a ghastly howl resounded throughout the castle walls.

"Eric's happy for you," the Seer sniggered. "Congratulations, gentlemen. May you always be deemed a credit by your brethren."

"They will be, when the king hears of their deeds," Roselyn said.

"They will be hanged from his gibbet," the Seer scowled, "unless they give more for their commendation than cavorting across the countryside, leading an army of Vikings. Stay your anger! You're both better than any knight I've met, but how will you claim to have earned this honor? Fighting giants, werewolves, murdering Grusshire, and infuriating the Earl of Northumbria?"

"We could kill a wizard," Karl sneered.

"Doubtful," the Seer scowled. "All I care about is: are you still coming with me?"

"We have to," Karl said. "For Eric's sake."

"And for Eloise," Rafe added.

"And for yourselves," the Seer said. "If you want the king to let you keep these titles, you'd best give him a reason. New knights go on a mission, to war, or present the king with a valuable gift. Isn't that right, Roselyn ...?"

"Yes, but surely our quest is daring enough," Roselyn argued.

"It is, but who'll witness it?" laughed the Seer. "You ...? Me ...? We're escaped criminals in the king's eyes."

"Then we'll prove it," Rafe said.

"How ...?" the Seer asked. "With a wild tale of ghosts and other worlds ...?"

"I see what you're saying," Karl said. "We have to bring back proof ... or we won't be believed."

"As long as you're still going," the Seer said, "I don't care about the rest."

"Worry about it in silence," Roselyn said. "You're spoiling our celebration. Seren, open up those packs and pass out dinner; I'm starving."

Their feast was delightful, heated over the baron's, now Eloise's, fireplace in a large pan Sarah had given them. Stashed in her pack, Eloise also found a bottle of Farmer Tiller's special liquor and passed it around. The Seer advised saving it, yet they could easily make more, so he was outvoted, and they drank and laughed until they were sotted.

"Speech ...!" Roselyn called as the first lights of dawn graced the barred windows. "Com'on, you virgin knights, give us a speech!"

"Yea!" Seren cried. "Speech to us ...!"

Rafe and Karl declined, but the others began chanting 'speech', so they staggered up to drunkenly lean against the hearth.

"I wan- I want you all to know," Karl slurred, "how grateful I am for .., for the honor you've given us."

"Me, too ...!" Rafe shouted.

"The glorious honor of knighthood, a dream whi(hic)ch I never ... something .., yet here I am, a knight."

"Me too," Rafe shouted, falling back against the fireplace stones.

"I want to promise ...," Karl said, "... I will be the ... best knight you ever drank with ..."

"Me too," Rafe said, starting to slide down.

"... and wif' my brother, Sir Rafe duuuu Harmonnn, I shall cut a path where there ain't one, because I love my brother Rafe."

"Me too," muttered Rafe, hitting bottom.

"It-It's getting b-b-bright outside," the Seer noticed.

"So ...?" Roselyn asked. "Can't leave 'til tonight."

"The, um, the baronon ... um, Eloise said she wanted to go to dem- Demril ... today."

"Well, let's go Demril ...!" Seren laughed, trying to stand up, half-fallen out of her clothes.

"No, it's bedtime!" Eloise shouted.

"The sssun is risssing, not sssinking," the Seer said.

"No!" Eloise cried. "We can't go like (burp) like this! Everybody to bed! Baronial orders!"

Laughing hysterically, Karl helped Seren pull Rafe up, and push him onto the bed, where he fell laughing. Then Eloise grinned widely, grabbed Karl by his wrist, and pulled him toward the door.

"Where ... we going?" Karl asked, stumbling.

"My room," Eloise said, swaying to keep from falling. "It's time I t-taught you your ... duties to your (hic) liege."

Stunned, Roselyn watched them vanish out of the doorway. She could say nothing; she'd made Eloise

Baroness to knight Karl and Rafe, mostly to thwart the Seer's leadership of their company. Roselyn never suspected Eloise would take other privileges.

She knew Karl; he would willingly succumb to her best friend.

Suddenly Roselyn felt cold and alone. She lowered her head, swaying; she was still drunk, yet Karl loved her, not Eloise.

Why did he go with her ...?

Rafe and Seren lay buried under blankets in the baron's bed, giggling and cuddling in the dark. They had each other, but Roselyn had no one.

Slowly Roselyn looked across the room, trying to focus her eyes. The Seer lay slumped on his divan. He was handsome enough, and she felt sorry for him at times. He'd endured a rough life, cast out by his own order. Roselyn's life had been equally difficult; she understood his bitterness, although not why he let it control him.

"Hey, Athelwynne!" Roselyn said. "W-Why you gotta be such a jerk all th' time?"

"I'mmm not a jerk!" the Seer protested. "It's just ... I got duties soooo important ... the Lady told me I gotta ..!"

"The Lady told you ...?" Roselyn asked, shaking her head to try and clear it, but only making herself dizzy. "W- What ...? When ...?"

"At night, in my dreams." the Seer said. "The Lady told me I gotta ..."

Roselyn rose up and crossed the room, stepping inside his circle of salt and looking down at him.

"What did (hic) you dream?" Roselyn asked.

"I dreamed .. the Lady told me I gotta ...," the Seer said.

"Aw, shuttup and kiss me," Roselyn said, and she pulled his face against hers. It was a sloppy kiss, but warm and sincere.

"B- But ... I thought ... you d-didn't like me," the Seer said.

"The Lady told me I gotta ...," Roselyn shrugged, and she kissed him again.

Chapter 10

Pain and Parades

ELOISE

Sunlight seared through Eloise's eyes. She reached for a pillow to bury her head.

It couldn't be morning; Eloise needed sleep: precious sleep, yet something was irritating, thwarting her return to slumber. Her pillow was missing; eye's closed, Eloise's searching hand touched flesh and wavy hair: Karl lay beside her, naked; no blankets covered either of them, yet something else, something bad, tugged at her.

Eloise slowly sat up, then clenched her teeth against a dizziness spinning her throbbing head. She and Karl were cuddled together on her huge bed, her blankets on the floor.

"Karl ...," Eloise groaned.

"He's dead," Karl groaned. "Oh, my stomach! My head! What was in that stuff?"

"Ask the Seer," Eloise spoke as her stomach suddenly growled. "I think I'm going to throw up."

Eloise leaped out of bed and made it to her window just as her stomach convulsed. Bile splashed down the castle's outer wall toward the courtyard. Eloise winced, spat, and continued. Soon a blanket wrapped around her, held by Karl; Eloise wished she felt well enough to be grateful.

An eternity later, Eloise staggered back and pulled her blanket tight around her. Karl was on his knees, looking under her bed.

"Eloise, where are our clothes?"

Eloise glanced about; Karl's mail, swordbelt, and boots were strewn just inside her door, but nowhere lay his gambeson, tunic, and trousers, or her dress.

Eloise vaguely remembered Karl chasing her down a narrow hallway, yet she couldn't remember where, and her head hurt too much to concentrate. With no recourse, they wrapped in blankets and went to search.

The hallway was empty, so they entered the main hall. Mostly it looked the same as usual; with sunlight beaming in through high windows. They searched every corner, yet found no clothes.

"Perhaps one of the others found them," Eloise suggested.

"I just hope Eric didn't abscond with them," Karl said. "He'd think it funny."

Seren laughed shrilly as Karl and Eloise entered the baron's room tightly clutching bedclothes. Wearing only Rafe's shirt, Seren sat on Eloise's throne, which she'd turned to face the fire, over which she was boiling water.

"You no look good," Seren smiled.

"Feel worse," Eloise said.

Eloise saw the divan and froze. From under a blanket poked two sets of naked feet: Roselyn's and the Seer's.

Eloise's mouth fell open. She'd dimly worried that Roselyn would be jealous of her taking Karl, afraid she'd restart their rivalry.

Eloise couldn't believe Roselyn had slept with the Seer.

Then Eloise looked at Karl's eyes, his mouth frozen in a silent gasp. His anguished expression melted like that of a beaten puppy whose master had just died, and his skin paled.

Eloise clenched her blanket tightly around her. *Karl loved Roselyn, but didn't he also love her?* Eloise suspected he did, yet ... did Karl sleep with her willingly ... or because he was drunk?

Whom would Karl have chosen to sleep with if Eloise hadn't ordered him to follow her ...?

"We have to go," Eloise said, seizing Karl's arm.

"Where ...?" Seren asked.

"To ... find our clothes."

Seren laughed again, and Eloise blushed as she yanked Karl toward the door.

The Seer was small and mean; *why did Roselyn sleep with him?* Roselyn couldn't love him; he was mildly handsome*, but still ...!*

Eloise led Karl down several familiar hallways, pointlessly searching ... mostly to keep Karl busy. Karl's jaw remained clenched, and he walked stiffly, yet confusion filled his eyes. Eloise didn't know whether to feel sorry for him or not; while Karl was chasing Eloise naked through dark hallways, he could hardly expect Roselyn to remain faithful.

Did Roselyn sleep with the Seer out of revenge, since Eloise had taken Karl ...? Or was Roselyn trying to prove that she didn't need Karl ...? Or was she trying to make him jealous ...?

Eloise shook her pounding head; she could question Roselyn's motives forever. She wasn't even sure how she felt about it, and feared what Karl might be thinking. Yet Karl remained silent and followed Eloise almost blindly.

A shred of gray cloth lay on the floor beside a stairs. Eloise lifted it up; it was a single sleeve of the dress Sarah Tiller had given her. Eloise looked down the hall and up the narrow staircase, yet no other sign of her dress or her brown apron showed. Absently she wondered what they'd been doing, how her sleeve had gotten torn, and what she was going to wear into town.

Eloise ascended the stairs partway, then stopped; from the light of a tiny window, Eloise saw the stairs blackened with a thick coating of dried blood. Someone had died here, probably during the siege. Eloise backed away, almost tripping on her blanket. The castle looked familiar, almost untouched, yet terrible things had happened here; signs of death probably lay all about.

"Let's go back," Eloise said to Karl.

Karl looked at her, then averted his tearing eyes. Eloise swallowed hard; *in his foul mood, she could lose him ...!*

"Let's go to my room," Eloise said.

As they entered Eloise's room, she glanced at her ransacked wardrobe and empty chest of drawers. She wondered where her dresses were; probably on a dragonship headed for Norway, where peasant women would fight over them in some backwater marketplace. The Vikings had left her nothing.

Eloise closed the door behind them, and then threw her blanket onto the bed and stood meekly before him, naked in the daylight.

Karl made love to Eloise like a wild animal, pounding his chest against hers. Eloise gasped and squealed, yet she urged him harder, faster. It didn't last long, yet their lovemaking was fierce and powerful. She bit back screams and let him ride her until he collapsed, spent. Then she held fast to him as if she'd never let go.

Much later, Eloise roused Karl. Afternoon showed in bright sunbeams sliding across her floor. Her head wasn't pounding anymore. Wrapped in blankets, they took a few deep breaths, and headed back to her father's room.

Roselyn and the Seer were dressed, sitting apart, with Rafe and Seren between them. No one laughed as they entered wearing blankets; all sat before the roaring fire, eating.

"Cabbage soup," Seren said. "Good. You want?"

"Please," Eloise said self-consciously. She wondered what her stepfather would think if he'd heard her speak politely to a tavern-slut.

Seren looked disgustingly happy, as if the liquor that had wiped them out hadn't affected her at all. Then Eloise remembered Seren's sickness in the swamp; foaming at the mouth while they held her down; Seren had grown up in a brothel and could probably out-drink them all.

"You look well," Eloise commented.

"I wake early," Seren said. "Explore. Never been in castle before. Drafty. Found bowls in kitchen. Not many; Vikings plunder all, except closet."

"What closet ...?" Eloise asked.

"There," Seren pointed at the back wall.

Eloise and Karl exchanged glances.

"The treasure room ...?" Roselyn asked.

"No treasure," Seren said. "Books, clothes, spears: much else."

"Clothes ...?" Eloise gasped.

Eloise hurried to the closet door and opened it wide. Haphazard piles lay everywhere, including a huge pile of dresses.

"My gowns ...!" Eloise shouted, so excited she lost her grip on her blanket; it fell to the floor before she could grab it and cover herself again. "Roselyn, your gowns are here, too, and father's garb; we have clean clothes again! Karl, help me!"

"What are those books?" the Seer asked, coming up from behind.

With the Seer's unexpected help, soon the baron's bed was covered with treasures from the closet. Roselyn chose a dress for herself, and then picked one that fit Seren. Eloise recognized some gowns from other castle women, elders probably long dead. Yet Eloise insisted they all wash before dressing. At Eloise's command, Rafe emptied the soup-pot into their bowls and left to wash out the pot and bring it back full of fresh water from the well.

"Look at this!" Karl said, holding up a light helmet. "There're swords in here ... and some armor."

"While Svenson chased us, whomever he left in charge of Bristlen probably gathered everything he could sell and stuffed it in that closet," the Seer said.

"Why not take it with them?" Karl asked.

"Eric, I guess," the Seer said. "I'll wager the Vikings left quickly when Eric arrived."

"What a sight that must have been!" Eloise chuckled. "Vikings running scared."

"Like we did when we first saw Eric's ghost," the Seer reminded.

Eloise smiled. Karl and the Seer were mostly ignoring each other, although neither smiled. It was better than she'd expected, as if Karl was pretending not to know whom Roselyn had slept with. Yet Karl's eyes burned with an intensity she'd never seen before.

Rafe returned with clean water, and hung the pot on the hook in the fireplace, and then fussed over new clothes and weapons. Rafe found a suit of mail that fit him just as the water started steaming.

"Ladies first," Eloise said, and she swung the strong hook out, away from the flames, and dipped a clean towel into the hot water. She started to drop her blanket, then looked up and saw all of the men watching her.

"Turn around ...!" Eloise ordered in her most imperious baronial tone.

Eloise, Roselyn and Seren stripped and wiped clean while the men stood silent, their backs to them. Eloise stole looks at Roselyn enviously; Roselyn's ample figure was far more developed than hers. Seren had the largest breasts, although hers sagged more. Actually, Seren looked younger naked, the lines on her body not nearly as numerous as the few wrinkles on her face.

When they let the men turn around, Eloise, Roselyn, and Seren stood properly dressed in shining court gowns. The Seer nodded approvingly, and Rafe lauded them with many compliments, yet Karl only frowned.

Despite orders to look away, the women laughingly snuck sly looks while the men bathed, receiving numerous complaints about unfair treatment. Eloise giggled as Karl protested; the men kept their backs to the women, which only made Eloise giggle harder. A lot of clothes were big enough for Rafe, but the clothes he'd selected proved too big to fit Karl. Eloise found for him a court guardsman's uniform, a short black tunic with matching hosen, and brought it to him. He snarled at her, but she only patted his naked butt and walked away.

For Rafe, Seren had chosen one of Eloise's stepfather's outfits, heavily-brocaded with royal blue stitching. Rafe complained of her choice, yet assented rather than argue. The Seer didn't wait for them to embarrass him, just shook out his black robes and redressed in them.

Before leaving, Karl and Rafe briefly searched the castle, yet they found little of use. Rotting corpses lay tucked into corners, and Karl reported that they tried not to look at them too closely. The only good things Karl found were three stout bows and seven quivers of arrows, which had been stacked in the watchtower over the gate. Rafe had found a heavy Viking axe, yet he refused to pull it out of the back of the Saxon it had killed.

The Seer took all of the books and scrolls, which seemed to have been Bristlen's library, and put them safely in a small chest, which he hid under the baron's bed.

The clothes Eloise and Karl were wearing when they'd arrived were never found.

Afternoon waned as they gathered to leave. Karl brushed their horses while Rafe hitched to his horse a small wagon once used for gathering peat, into which they put two large chests, one with two extra suits of mail, the armor Roselyn had stolen from her father, some kitchen wares, and five wool blankets. The other chest was stuffed with clothes.

Rafe's suit of mail wasn't riveted or silvered like Karl's, yet he wore it proudly. He and Karl also wore their shields and the packs Farmer Tiller had given them, still full of food and supplies.

"We'd best not be going far," Rafe laughed. "Women always over-pack."

They were hungry again, yet they wanted to spare their supplies; they rode laughing out of Bristlen, shouting farewells to Eric; they'd seen no sign of him all morning.

Only Rafe's skill as a horsemaster kept their tiny wagon under control as they rode the treacherous path down to Demril. Below them, the church bell rung out, and a few folk came out of ruined homes to watch them descend.

Eloise felt terrible, looking down on the remains of Demril: half-blackened buildings, many with charred, collapsed roofs. The devastation wasn't as bad as Grusshire, yet this was her village, the town above which she'd grown up.

Four great dragonships still floated in the harbor, tethered yet abandoned. Eloise smiled; Svenson and his fallen army needed no more ships.

A crowd had gathered by the time they reached Demril's streets. Some of the townsfolk seemed glad to see them, others less so, yet none spoke against them since Karl and Rafe wore weapons, a strange priest rode with them, and the women wore fine gowns.

Without addressing the peasants, Eloise rode straight to the steps of the church; grumbling townsfolk followed. Eloise had assumed her pious air of royalty, and the questions shouted at her went unheeded.

On the church steps stood a young priest she'd never seen.

"Where's Father Jorden?" Eloise asked.

"With God," the young priest said bitterly. "Vikings slew him on his altar."

Eloise paused, bowing her head.

"My sympathies," Eloise said. "I'll see that a worthy contribution is made to afford him masses in perpetuity. I've just returned from Madrone, where

Svenson's Viking army fell like wheat under vengeful Saxon hands."

"We heard about that already, Lady du Harmonn," a stout older man said angrily, and he limped forward on a staff. "The army of Sir Guldwin, Earl of Northumbria, slaughtered them over two weeks ago."

"I was there," Eloise said. "It was no easy battle, as members of my guard can attest, since one of their brothers died there. Where's the rest of Demril?"

"We're all that's left," the older man shouted, shaking his staff threateningly. "All of the others died or fled."

"My grief is multiplied," Eloise said, bowing her head. "My father vanished the night of the siege and hasn't been found."

"I'll tell you what happened to your father," the old man said. "On a pole, they hung him over the battlements at dawn, and then they let him drop, and good riddance! He should've protected us when the Vikings ...!"

"Hold your tongue, dog!" Karl shouted. "Don't forget to whom you speak! With the Baron fallen, his title and powers fall upon his only child, who'd order me to cleave your fat head were she not grieving so. Find you pleasure in tormenting a young girl orphaned?"

"My wife was beaten while I lay injured and helpless, and then carried up into Bristlen, from where she never came out," the old man said, leaning heavily on his staff. "Tire not my ears with tales of your suffering."

"Vikings caused grief to us all," Eloise said.

"Why did they come ...?" a stout man demanded. "What did they bring such an army ...? We had nothing, unless they cared only to spill blood!"

"Who knows such things?" Eloise asked. "We've all suffered, but those whom we've lost have been avenged. Now it's time to rebuild. We each have work to do. Father, would you take charge in my absence, and see that each of these good folk claim one house still remaining, and when I return, I'll verify their claims."

"We don't need your verifications, missy!" the old man hissed.

"Cur ...!" Karl cried, and he drew his sword and rose it over his head. *"Respect your baroness ... or I'll kill you ...!"*

"No!" Eloise ordered. "I'll see no more blood stain my land."

Karl relented, yet kept his sword in hand.

The old man subsided, cowed, yet he continued to glare.

"As I was saying," Eloise continued, nodding slightly to Karl, "Demril will be rebuilt. We'll be away shortly, securing funds for its reconstruction. Please spare no labor. You, young priest, shall watch and keep tally. Those who work hardest shall receive the most when I return, and those with prior claims or inheritance due must hold their claims until funds are arranged.

"Unfortunately, young priest, we may be expecting a ... uh, ... messenger from the king, so we can't leave until dusk. Have you fare enough to share an evening meal? Our own supply runs low, and we've far to travel ere it may be replenished."

"The Vikings left us little," the priest said.

"Then we'll share what you have," Karl insisted.

"Demril won't starve," Eloise said. "I've made arrangements with a wealthy farmer who'll sell us whatever resources Demril needs, which is why I must leave so soon, to get back before the local stores are used up."

"Where are you going?" the young priest asked.

"I'd rather that not be known," Eloise said. "Bristlen needs much restoration, which is costly. I hope to secure a loan, and I wouldn't have word of my errand reach there before I do."

"Ha- Have you been there?" a young boy asked. "They say that the dead haunt Bristlen."

"They do ...!" the Seer warned, his voice low and threatening. "Beware of Bristlen! Stay away from the castle, if you value your life!"

Eloise grinned; the Seer was thinking only of his hidden library.

"Vikings certainly thought so," the young priest said. "Scared like rabbits they left, running for their boats. One of their brethren was seen jumping off the battlements, screaming of ghosts. Around midnight, they just ran to their ships and sailed away. God's will it was;

the heathens were making themselves quite at home in Bristlen."

"Is the chapel open?" Eloise asked. "I have much to pray for, and perhaps little time before I must leave."

"The house of God is always open," the young priest asserted.

Eloise began to dismount, and Rafe hurried to help her down. Karl sheathed his sword and slid off, assisted Roselyn and Seren to dismount, and then helped Rafe tie their horses to a post. The crowd started to disperse, having witnessed all they could.

"No heathens enter the Lord's house!" the priest cried suddenly, blocking the Seer's entrance.

"God made the forests and fields," the Seer smiled. "This house was built by men."

"Dare you mock the Lord ...?" the priest challenged.

"No, merely his foolish servant. Now step aside, or would you deny your services to one who serves the Lady?"

"Your Lady is a witch in league with the devil!"

"Nonsense," the Seer said. "Your devils are certainly not in Her league, but I'd gladly hear more about this Jesus the Jew. I've heard much rumor, yet little fact."

"He wasn't a Jew!" the priest argued.

"His parents were," the Seer said, "but doorways are no place for debate. Come, let's talk inside."

"But ... you're a heathen!"

"God has forgiven far worse," the Seer replied, and he calmly took the young priest's arm and led him inside.

Eloise entered the chapel, strode to its front, and knelt against the communion rail. Roselyn and Seren joined her. Karl walked up, knelt beside Roselyn, and winked at Eloise.

"You do need to pray," Karl whispered. "That was the longest string of lies I've ever heard; I thought you were Eric."

"Should I have told him the truth?" Eloise grinned.

"No, but what now?"

"Keep the priest busy getting food ready," Roselyn said. "He'll be manageable as long as we kneel here. Let him and the Seer argue; it'll keep him from asking questions."

"I give priest good confession," Seren offered.

"No ...!" Eloise and Roselyn hissed together, trying not to giggle.

"Why not?" Karl smirked. "Just let me tie him down first ... so we can watch his face!"

Chapter 11

Sad Sailors

KARL

Upon the back pew, Karl found Rafe, sitting and frowning. Karl glared at the Seer, wanting only to kill him.

How could Roselyn have slept with him ...?

Imaginings of him and Roselyn lying naked under a blanket tormented. Karl's hand flexed as if eager to grip his sword. Yet Eric and Eloise's only hopes would be lost without the Seer, so Karl seethed silently. For their sakes, he couldn't lose control.

"That priest isn't the smartest," Karl commented.

"Old Father Jorden was a far wiser man," Rafe nodded. "This new priest ..., well, he'll grow and learn, as we all do."

"I'm surprised you're not praying with the ladies."

"I trust in God more than anything ... except that those villagers will steal our horses, given a chance."

"Go. I'll watch the horses."

"Thanks," Rafe smiled. "You don't believe in God much, do you?"

"I believe in something," Karl said. "I just don't know what. Before Titania, I'd never seen proof of any religion. Now I have faith in the Lady, but that doesn't mean I don't believe in God. I guess I just don't worry about it."

"Someday you may need to choose," Rafe said.

"Someday, perhaps," Karl said. "I don't see why you worry now."

"With God, I don't need to worry," Rafe smiled, patted Karl's shoulder, and then walked to the communion rail and knelt beside Seren.

Karl sat and watched the horses, fingering his golden ribbon, and wondering about Rafe's words. If there was a God, then what was Titania, whose token he wore? The Seer's powers were indisputable; the Druid Lady had to be real, yet the Seer was leading them to the land of Eric's Norse Gods. Were all Gods, Rafe's, Eric's, and the Seer's, in league with each other ...? Or were they competitors, and if so, what did they compete for ...?

Karl shrugged; he was a knight, more than he'd ever thought possible. If Karl knew the answers to these questions, he'd be a Pope.

Why had Roselyn slept with the Seer ...?

She'd made Karl swear to obey Eloise, and then said nothing when Eloise ordered him into her bedchamber.

Guilt welled; Karl didn't have to obey Eloise. He'd deserted Roselyn, left her alone with that slimy Seer. He was to blame.

Why did she do it ...?

Amid their ecclesiastical conversation, the young priest and the Seer carried in a large table and set it behind Karl's pew beside the open door. Karl glanced to make sure no one was near their horses, and then he helped carry in three chairs and turn the last pew around. Soon they all sat down to eat.

After the prayer, the Seer and the priest's arguments gave them all a headache. The watery onion stew had barely enough meat to cover a rat's bones, yet they ate ravenously as shadows grew long outside.

"You must excuse us, Father," Eloise said suddenly. "It's getting late, and I wish to inspect the Viking ships before sunset. There're some who'll pay well for such vessels, you know."

"You'll have to talk to the townsmen," the priest said. "Some have already claimed those ships."

"By what right …?" Eloise asked.

"That's no business of mine, but those Vikings had two dozen ships here, each with a guard. Eleven ships were left after they fled. Seven have already vanished, probably sold by sailors. The ones that remain have been claimed."

"I determine claims inside my barony," Eloise asserted, and she glanced outside. "It's getting dark. I must inspect my ships, and my companions must join me; I won't travel without escort."

"Very well," the priest said. "I'll get my cloak and come with you."

"No need!" the Seer laughed, standing up. "Don't go into the cold for our sake. Stay here and pray for my heathen soul, and perhaps I'll try praying with you when we return."

The priest tried to argue, yet they quickly departed. From the chests on their wagon, they put on the cloaks Farmer Tiller had given them, then took their horses, and led them on foot.

Demril's docks were deserted, save for the eerie creaks of the ghostly ships bumping against gray wooden posts. As the sun set, they dismounted and stood in a circle, waiting.

Suddenly their horses neighed and stamped, skittish and agitated. Roselyn gasped, and a shivering chill gripped Karl. The Seer took out his magic moonstone.

Eric glowed into view on the end of the dock. Cautiously all stepped back, but they couldn't flee. Hauntingly Eric's glowing form wavered, oblivious to wind or cold. His tormented expression revealed all.

"Lead us, Eric, and we'll follow," the Seer said.

Somberly Eric walked off the edge of the pier, out onto invisible air, and then he slowly sank onto the water's surface, where he continued his sad trek, his glowing prints floating behind him on the waves.

"Well, let's go," the Seer said happily.

"Go where ...?" Karl asked loudly to be heard over the wind.

"After Eric, of course," the Seer grinned. "Choose a boat and get our stuff aboard."

"Do you know how to sail a dragonship?" Karl asked incredulously.

"Can't think of a better time to learn," the Seer smiled.

Karl turned to Rafe, wondering if he'd heard wrong.

"Don't look at me," Rafe said. "I've done a little sailing, but nothing like this."

"Do we have a choice?" Roselyn asked, and she began unsaddling her horse.

"I'm not going out to sea in that thing ...!" Karl shouted. "None of us know how to sail it, and a storm's coming."

"Unload the wagon, my knights," Eloise ordered with a knowing smile, and she unstrapped her horse's bridle.

"Relax!" the Seer laughed. "If this is the worst we face on this quest, we'll be lucky indeed!"

Madness, Karl thought, yet Rafe took his arm and pulled him back towards the cart.

"Come on, Sir Karl. No use arguing now."

As they loaded, the wind tore at their skin, cloaks, and garb. When done, they left their unburdened horses by the dock and cast off, sorry to see them go, yet none wanted to sail a horse-ladened ship to only-gods-know-where.

Rafe tested the lines, trying to figure out the rigging, while Karl and the Seer plied with the heavy oars. The dragonship seemed reluctant to move, yet slowly they drifted away from the dock, rocking ungently.

Karl wanted to jump ship and swim for shore while he had the chance, but Rafe called for him to help raise the sail, and he acquiesced.

Karl's chilled hands screamed against the burning rope, but slowly, with his and Rafe's weight combined, they hoisted the heavy sail and secured it. The wind filled it instantly, puffed out its striped canvas, and the ship lurched sideways and tilted precariously.

"Someone, man the rudder!" Rafe shouted.

Eloise, too small to lift much, ran to the carven tail. She grabbed the tiller and pulled with all of her strength; the ship foundered, and the wind pushed them closer to shore.

"Turn! Turn! We're going the wrong way!" Rafe shouted.

Rafe reset the lines and turned the mighty sail. Eloise pulled at the tiller with all of her might, yet their ship turned the opposite way, its prow facing the dock. Laughing, the Seer went back to help Eloise while Rafe, Roselyn and Karl fought to turn the sail again.

Seren clung to the side, terrified.

"I no swim …!" Seren cried.

An hour passed before Karl felt safe. They still hadn't left the harbor, yet Rafe and the Seer worked as a team, and tacked them toward open sea. In that hour, Karl learned more about sailing than any of them had previously known.

Shouts from the village priest reached their ears against the wind; alone he stood upon the dock, watching them depart Demril Harbor.

The night was black and miserable. The girls huddled by the mast, wrapped in windswept cloaks, while Karl stood in the prow, shivering, watching for rocks below the black water's surface. Freezing winds stung his chapped face and blew back his hood. Karl frowned; *sooner or later they'd sink …!*

Fortunately, unless they did sink, things couldn't get worse.

Rain started to spatter the deck.

Rain had good points; the wind eased up and the harbor waters relaxed.

Slowly they rounded the breakwater; up and down they lurched, rolling in the surf, and Seren and Eloise both were sick over the sides. Roselyn tried to comfort them, holding her cloak over their heads to keep off the drenching rain and chill. The Seer said something to them, and then approached Karl.

"How are they ...?" Karl shouted through the downpour.

"Just seasick!" the Seer shouted back. *"How're we doing ...?"*

"How should I know ...?" Karl cried.

"Seen any rocks ...?"

"No."

"Then we're doing fine. Rafe says that we'll be past this soon. Move out of my way."

Karl stepped aside, and the Seer pulled out his moonstone and held it up. No glowing marks appeared on the rain-spattered water. The Seer looked frustrated, put his moonstone away, and then opened a secret compartment in the bow that Karl had been sitting atop. Inside it lay another sail.

"What's that for ...?" Karl shouted.

"Ask Rafe," the Seer shouted back. *"He wants it."*

It wasn't a sail. While the Seer held the tiller, Rafe tied the heavy cloth to the rails, all the way up and back, covering the rain-wet deck. Then Rafe found narrow staves stashed by the stern and set them at intervals underneath, upholding the cloth like a tent-roof. Roselyn got Eloise and Seren underneath canvas tarp while Rafe, the Seer, and Karl held a meeting by the stern, huddled close so each could hear.

"We could tie off the tiller and let the wind carry us out to sea," Rafe said.

"The wind could change direction," Karl argued.

"Not tonight," the Seer said. "It'll blow toward land until dawn. We'll have to come out to check periodically, but we can wait inside."

"Why are we doing this?" Karl asked. "We don't know where we're going. Eric's tracks floated on the water, but the rain's destroyed them. We'll get lost!"

"We've no choice," the Seer said. "Once we're out to sea, if we don't find any signs, we'll turn north. Eric is headed to Valhalla, part of the Norse faith; chances are any entrance to their realm will be near Norse lands. We should cross Eric's path somewhere."

"We'll make it," Rafe said. "This isn't a big storm. It'd be more dangerous trying to sail back to the dock."

Inside the damp canvas covering, after they got settled, the Seer dug a candle out of one of their packs. Holding it in both hands, the Seer went into a deep trance, and suddenly the candle sparked ablaze. All jumped as the tiny light blinded them, yet didn't ask how he'd done it.

Candlelight revealed all looking like drowned cats, scraggly-haired, unhappy, and soaked. Yet inside the awning felt safe, almost cozy, hidden from the rain and wind.

The Seer went out every now and then to check the ship's direction and look of signs of Eric. He reported that all sounds of surf had vanished; they were far out to sea.

"Well, at least we don't have to ride any more horses for a while," Roselyn said. "My ... saddle hurt."

"At least, if you fall off your horse, you can stand up where you land," Rafe said.

"What if sink ...?" Seren asked.

"Listen," Karl said, yawning. "It's been a long day and tomorrow may be worse. Let's just blow out the candle and get some sleep."

Karl awoke in darkness. He was snuggled between Roselyn and Eloise with Rafe and Seren's legs lying across his, on and under all the dry blankets and cloaks they had. From their combined body-heat, Karl was baking, and sore from sleeping on a tossing deck. Karl quietly slipped out, careful not to disturb.

The Seer was standing in the bow, staring at the moon, which seemed huge, but no longer full. What they'd do if Eloise transformed aboard ship Karl shuddered to think about.

The Seer seemed lost in his own thoughts. It'd stopped raining; the sea was calm, the breeze blowing strongly. Karl glared at the Seer; *where was his sword when he needed it?*

"He's gone," the Seer said sadly, not even looking at him. "Eric's gone, and we're lost."

Karl wanted to push him overboard. The image of the Seer's naked feet sticking out from under a blanket beside Roselyn's infuriated him. The Seer wasn't as smart as he pretended; none of the company had died before the Seer forced himself upon them.

But, good as it might feel, Karl couldn't push Seer overboard; *to sleep with Eloise, Karl had abandoned Roselyn.*

"We'll find Eric," Karl said, struggling to sound hopeful.

"This was my one chance," the Seer said. "I blew it."

The Seer's unexpected familiarity surprised Karl.

"How so?"

"I should've kept us in Castle Bristlen until fairer weather."

"There's no fairer weather than spring," Karl said. "Storms happen all year round on the coast. We're alive, and the rain's stopped. We'll find Eric."

"Perhaps," the Seer said. "If we were to sail north during the day, when Eric's tracks are pale, and then tack east and west at night, we should be able to see some trace. But it'd take a long time; our food won't last."

"We can fish."

The Seer shrugged his shoulders.

"Why're you doing this?" Karl asked. "We're doing this for Eric and Eloise. Why are you?"

"Only men of faith would understand," the Seer said. "Rafe does. My Lady has some high purpose planned; it's not for me to question Her will."

"We'll find Eric," Karl shrugged. "If not, when we get to Norway, I'll kill another Viking ... and we can follow him to Eric."

The Seer smiled, trying not to chuckle.

Chapter 12

Freedom

ROSELYN

Roselyn awoke to the gentle rocking of the waves. She stretched and yawned loudly; very unlady-like, but she didn't care.

Roselyn was free ... finally ...!

Since they'd cast off from Demril's dock, Roselyn had felt released. Earl Sir Guldwin ruled most of Northern England, but not the sea, and Roselyn wasn't in England anymore. She was finally away, and somehow she knew she'd never go back. Roselyn would never again see her father's face, never serve as his royal whore ... or suffer his fists.

Roselyn opened her eyes to see horizontal wooden slats upholding the awning over her. Eloise was sleeping beside her, and Rafe and Seren were both snoring, enmeshed in each other's arms. Roselyn smiled; she hoped someone would hold her all night when she was old and gray.

Missing Karl, Roselyn sat up and saw, outside the awning, Karl's boots standing beside the black hem of the Seer's robe. She hoped they were working things out: Karl had barely spoken to her since she'd slept with the Seer, and she couldn't blame him. Roselyn still didn't know why she'd done it, except that she'd been drunk and had thought it would keep the company together.

Or had she been defying Eloise ...?

There was more to Athelwynne than she'd suspected; the Seer was insufferable, yet Roselyn sensed that someone else lay hidden inside him, buried behind the facade of the angry Druid outcast. An evil man wouldn't have forgiven them after Grusshire; the Seer was bitter, but inside ... something sweet slept.

Roselyn extended her arms wide and stretched again.

Free ...!

"Hey ...!" Eloise complained, pushing at Roselyn's foot.

"Sorry."

"Where are we?"

"Who knows? Who cares? We're away from England. Away ...!"

Eloise sat up.

"I'm still a baroness, and you're a countess," Eloise said.

"In the past," Roselyn said. "What do titles matter here?"

"I didn't sleep well," Eloise said. "I feel ... uneasy. Du Harmonn is my barony, and I'm deserting my people. Mother wanted me to rule in her place, and now that I'm baroness ..."

"My father was going to imprison you until he could marry you to one of his bastard sons," Roselyn said. "You've no troops, and even if you defended Castle Bristlen, Father would've marched his army, besieged you, and taken your barony by force."

"He wouldn't dare!" Eloise said. "The king ...!"

"With you dead and my father's troops in command of Bristlen, the king would've demanded a huge ransom for the deed to du Harmonn, which my father would've paid by taxing your peasants," Roselyn said. "You don't know him; he wants all of Northumbria, and once he owns the north, he'll want the south, and then Scotland and Ireland."

"He wants to be a Caesar," Eloise frowned. "Not in my barony; I have to go back!"

"How can you stop him? He doesn't care about daughters, except how he can use you to gain and keep du Harmonn."

"There must be a way," Eloise said. "There has to be ...!"

Roselyn frowned. Eloise should forget her baronial claim, yet Roselyn knew she wouldn't; Eloise would always feel miserable if she didn't somehow rule du Harmonn as her mother had wanted.

Rafe yawned and blinked. Seren lay cuddled against him; deftly he untwined himself.

"How are we doing?" Rafe asked.

Roselyn and Eloise exchanged confused glances.

"The ... ship ...?"

Neither girl knew; Rafe chuckled, shook his head, and crawled out of the awning to survey their situation.

Roselyn chagrined, feeling foolish; again the men were doing all of the work, while she and Eloise were unaware what was getting done; asking about the condition of their ship, their course, or their mission had never occurred to her. With a glance at Eloise, Roselyn crawled out of the blankets and went to join the men.

"We've been turning the sail with the wind, but not the rudder," Karl said.

Rafe nodded approval.

"The compass says we're heading northwest," the Seer said. "I think we should turn north."

"Let's go a little farther in this direction," Rafe said. "A few more hours, and then we'll turn. We can't get too close to land; we don't have the experience to sail around reefs and sand bars."

Roselyn pushed out from under the canopy into a strong, cold wind. Wide ocean with small white caps stretched in every direction. The men were braced against the sides of the boat, the Seer almost hanging from a rope running from the large wooden tail to the sail. Roselyn staggered as the ship rocked; Karl and Rafe caught her before she fell.

The Seer caught her eye and smiled at her. Roselyn froze; *she'd made a mistake in Castle Bristlen, but how could she explain that?* Her reasons failed in the light of sobriety. Roselyn loved Karl, yet she couldn't insult the Seer in front of everybody and keep the peace. She forced herself to smile back.

"How long are we going to leave the canopy up?" Karl asked.

"Seren's still asleep," Rafe said.

"Can't we leave part of it up?" the Seer asked. "This wind'll rip our skins right off."

"We could leave the canopy over the bow," Rafe said.

"Where ...?"

"The front half; we can man the tiller and set the rigging from here."

Roselyn felt foolish, understanding little of their conversation. She wanted to help, yet had no idea what to do.

"Is anybody hungry ...?" she asked.

Roselyn crawled back inside the canopy, out of the wind. Chilled, she slipped back under the warm blankets beside Seren and Eloise, who'd gone back to sleep. Then she reached for their packs.

Something pinched Roselyn and made her jump; beneath her, the loose deck-boards shifted and rattled. She hoped the whole ship wasn't built this poorly or they'd certainly sink. Roselyn tested one of the wobbling floorboards; it actually lifted up completely.

Underneath it was a large, empty space. Roselyn looked carefully, then lifted up another board, surprised to find all the boards lifted. Under the deck, Roselyn spied something odd: a small wooden keg.

Waking up Eloise and Seren, who snarled sleepily and clutched her blankets tightly, Roselyn pulled up more floorboards. Coiled ropes and wooden boxes lay tightly packed under the deck-beams, with long oars and other things she couldn't identify.

Food ...! One large basket was lined with burlap and filled with grain. Another had walnuts, and one chest was full of small onions and leeks, and there were three large pumpkins and a sack of barley. Several small kegs of beer and bottles of wine lay nestled among the supplies.

Roselyn lifted up another floorboard and found ... dirt. Pulling out more beams, she found a firepit, a large square of packed dirt, about six inches deep. In the center of the dirt were the ashes of a fire.

"Why ...?" Eloise asked.

"Dirt no burn ... unlike ship," Seren explained.

"Let's pull up the rest," Roselyn said. "The Vikings must have firewood somewhere."

"Maybe we should thank them," Eloise laughed.

"Stores for all summer," Seren assumed. "Much good."

"Let's start breakfast," Roselyn said. "The men think they're doing all the work; let's see what they say when we serve beer with their first meal."

The men were delighted; the women found wooden mugs, and presented them brimming beside plates of cold sausage and cheese. All crawled under the canopy to eat, and the Seer decided to inventory their newfound supplies right away. Rafe insisted on having some walnuts and proudly grinned as he crushed their shells in his bare hands.

The day grew warm. Near noon, the men turned their vessel north. The choppy sea had eased, and the sun was bright and high. Despite the wind, it was warm on deck, and Rafe and Karl unlashed half of the canopy, leaving only the foredeck covered. They sat aft, passing around a clay bottle of strong mead, and finally relaxed.

The ship had another luxury Roselyn hadn't expected; with little privacy, neither the Seer nor Karl could force an intimate conversation she didn't want to have.

The Seer pulled out his moonstone several times and held it high, careful not to drop it into the sea. No yellow 'V's appeared.

Eventually Rafe and Seren crawled under the canopy and pulled the excess canvas over its entrance like a curtain. No one said anything, but soon they were all trying to ignore rhythmic grunts and muted exclamations.

"Exactly where are we going?" Roselyn asked the Seer, hoping to cover the sounds with conversation.

"He doesn't know," Karl said.

"How could I ...?" the Seer asked. "This 'crack in the world' is a passage only the dead use."

"Can living people use it?" Eloise asked.

"I assume so," the Seer said. "Titania spoke of fairies using it. Eric will find it, and we'll follow him through."

"What's on the other side?" Roselyn asked.

"Only the Lady knows," the Seer said. "It's a world beyond ours. Norse legends describe seas, mountains, and rivers, so I suspect we won't be far out of reckoning."

"You know Norse legends?" Roselyn asked.

"I had two eddas in my library in Madrone," the Seer said, and he frowned. "I wonder what happened to them; probably burned, or sold at market along with all my other books. Sir Guldwin doesn't read much, I suppose?"

"He can read," Roselyn said. "He has a large library, almost forty books, but I doubt if he's read many of them."

"I pray my books are safe," the Seer said. "If they're whole, I should be able to find them when I get back to Madrone; my life's research is in those books."

"So, what are Norse legends?" Eloise asked.

"Fables and stories," the Seer said. "Children's tales, I'd call the early ones, for they make little sense. There is this great tree, named Yggdrasil, which is the foundation of their universe."

"A tree ...?"

"A vast tree, big enough to hold entire nations in its branches," the Seer said. "See what I mean about children's tales? There was also a great cow, and a fearsome giant, who was the summit of all evil, and a man, who was all good."

Roselyn winced at the word 'giant'; she didn't want to see any more of those.

"Somehow they had sons and daughters; the text wasn't very clear how. Then the evil giant kills the good man, and the man's three grandsons avenge their kin by killing the giant. The man's oldest grandson was Odin, who became King of the Gods. The rest is mostly about wars between the Gods and the giants. There's an evil God, Loki, and he spawns all sorts of monsters and causes most of the havoc they face. Why the other Gods put up with Loki I don't know, but in the end, he betrays them. I read those books a long time ago, so I don't remember each story, but theirs is a strange world, full of bed-story creatures: greedy dwarves, fierce trolls, and dark elves, whatever they are."

They plied the Seer with questions, most of which went unanswered, and then the topic turned to other things. Karl pointed out to Eloise how the ship was rigged, and how they steered it and kept its sails full.

"Rafe figured it out," Karl said, and he got up to make an adjustment to the sail lines while they watched.

The afternoon dragged on, and the sun became hot, yet the breeze cooled them off. Rafe and Seren re-emerged, Rafe trying not to grin like a youth, yet utterly failing. Seren laughed and teased him.

That night, Rafe and the Seer argued about direction. Farmer Tiller's sextant and compass showed their position and direction, but they were useless without a map; they argued long over what the readings meant. Karl refused to take sides; it didn't matter to him which part of the ocean they sank in. Rafe and the Seer finally compromised; they turned the ship northeast, a direction neither preferred. Yet they saw was no sign of Eric.

That night, mostly because he was bored, Karl carved shavings from the stored firewood and lit a small fire on the dirt firepit. The light brightened them all, yet they couldn't raise the flames because the canvas would burn, and soon it became too smoky to enjoy. Karl lit two candles from it and put the fire out.

Roselyn realized the other problem with life on ship; while they had little privacy, they also had little to do. Rafe did most of the work, so they began calling him

Captain Sir Rafe until it became a game. Karl alone didn't call Rafe Captain Sir; Roselyn recalled that Karl had wanted that title in the inn, but they'd nicknamed him The Jester.

The women retired early. Inside the awning, they wrapped up in all the blankets and let the waves rock them to sleep. Roselyn curled up against Eloise for warmth, yet wished she could cuddle with Karl ... and wondered if he'd let her.

Chapter 13

Memories

ERIC

Eric glanced down at the sea rolling beneath his feet; foamy spray and splashes passed right through him, and deep watery troughs opened up beneath him, although he only floated over them, as if they belonged to another world. He couldn't feel any wind, which had to be blowing hard since it tossed countless airborne droplets. Above him shined countless stars, which Eric knew as well as any man alive, so he recognized that he was heading north, but whatever speed he was making was a mystery.

His ghostly form trekked slowly over the waves. No landmasses marked his progress; as far as Eric knew, the current could be dragging him anywhere. *Could current affect his death-march?* Eric had no way to tell.

His destination was undeniable; Eric could see, and hear (a little, as if hands were pressed tightly over his ears), yet the only sensation Eric felt was soulless desolation and his distant, final destination: the ultimate pit of despair. When Eric turned his head, he could sense when he was facing his doom.

He wondered where his companions were. He'd seen their dragonship follow him out of Demril Harbor but, lost in the rain, they'd sailed right past him. He'd tried to signal them, yet they couldn't see him. Now they were gone; Eric could only continue and hope they found him.

Valhalla ...!

The Seer's words had met Eric's ears like sweet air to a drowning man. Eric had felt a faint twinge of hope, yet it quickly faded. In the courtyard of Castle Bristlen, he'd understood enough of their words to press on, hoping beyond hope. His friends were still trying to save him; if not, he'd have simply lain down and faded, which would seem like another death. Keeping to his path seemed exhausting, yet Eric wouldn't give up until his very last hope failed.

Death without being chosen by the Valkyrie was everything Eric had feared. Eric's whole life had become meaningless in one vengeful stroke by Svenson

Two-Sword. Stories would be made about their final duel, and Eric wondered how he'd be portrayed; probably as the betrayer, Svenson's Royal Champion who killed his king's son and led a Viking army on a futile chase, only to fall beside his king's corpse in a pointless war that cost the lives of seven thousand Vikings; funny how twisted history became when written by those who didn't live it.

Memory was the only treasure Eric had left. Unwillingly, Eric recalled how it all began, at the celebration before the spring Viking.

* * * * * * * * * * *

Eric turned away from the roaring crowd after they'd shouted 'Svenson!' for the third time. Eric hated standing pompously behind Svenson's throne, and suffered presentations only when ceremony demanded. As Royal Champion, Eric had to attend his king while he sacrificed the bull to Odin for success in the annual Viking, yet Eric didn't have to stay for the celebration. The slain bull had already been piled atop its massive wooden bier, which Svenson had set alight, around which the warriors would dance and cheer all night. Yet Eric was too old and dignified for such foolishness; he headed toward Gunthar's Alehouse at his first opportunity.

Eric ducked as some drunk stumbled toward him with horns on his helmet. Damn fool: he could put someone's eye out with those useless ornaments. Horns on a helmet were stupid; a sudden blow could twist your head off, and only fools wore armor with handles. Eric let him be: fools who seek death are scorned by the Valkyrie. If any man dared to board Svenson's dragon wearing a horned helmet then Eric would tear it off and toss it overboard; it would give the rowers something to laugh about.

Eric glanced back for one last look at the festivities: King Svenson Two-Sword sat smiling on his high-backed walnut throne, while his only son, Thorland, stood between him and the sky-reaching fire. Fist raised, Thorland led the cheers, and drank as fast as he could. A wide, clear ring surrounded the sacrificial bonfire, which was already wafting enough heat to singe the light hairs of Thorland's thin, scraggily beard.

Hundreds of warriors cheered, from hardened swordmasters to bare-chinned youths excited about their first Viking. Traditionally, the Viking marked the end of spring; the fields were planted, the men eager to abandon their wives for the summer. Svenson always whipped his men into a fervor on their last night in Norway, the memory of which would sustain them during the dreary summer nights.

Eric pushed through the thinning crowd. No sign hung over Gunthar's door; those who didn't know where it was weren't welcome.

All eyes turned as Eric entered; true Norsemen never allowed strangers at their backs. Most of the elders were crowded around the big fireplace on chairs and benches, leaning back against sturdy tables. A few heads nodded greetings toward Eric before they turned back to stare into the flames. Eric closed the door behind him, glad to be out of the chaotic celebration.

Gunthar's alehouse looked the same as always; a wide longhouse with several tables, benches, and chairs, the greasy smoke of oil lamps wafting silently upwards, and huge kegs stacked against the back wall. A single oiled-lambskin window glowed dimly from the light of the bonfire outside. Inside, shadows offered comfortable, quiet familiarity.

"Eric ...!" Gunthar's toothless smile greeted him. "Come for a wet throat before the Viking?"

"All I can afford," Eric shrugged, yet he managed a smile as he reached into his pouch and pulled out his last few coppers. He handed them to Gunthar, who quietly pocketed them.

"Help yourself to the taps," Gunthar said. "You'll come back from the Viking with chests of gold again, no doubt."

Eric tried not to smile. He'd probably survive and profit again, as he had every year since he was young. Yet Eric wasn't young anymore. His joints ached in the mornings, and it seemed to take longer to rouse him every day. His position as Svenson's Champion protected him from most risks, and favored him with the best booty, but it wasn't comfort Eric sought.

Before the kegs, Eric pulled his ale-horn out of its leather loop on his wide belt. One keg had a grease-lamp before it; Eric held his ale-horn over the drip pan, turned the spigot, and filled his horn with Gunthar's potent brew.

In the shadows, sitting alone, Thorin Stormgard sat wrapped in his black cloak, drinking from his enormous tankard. Of all the elders, Thorin was the wisest and most respected. Eric had always held him in great esteem, although they'd seldom spoken; Thorin had been the Royal Champion of Svenson's father; Eric had taken that honor from him when Svenson assumed the throne. But, for what Eric needed, Thorin was the best.

Boldly Eric walked over uninvited, pulled out a small bench, and sat at Thorin's table. Thorin glared at him yet said nothing; Eric was trodding on dangerous ground, but he was resolved.

"I need advice," Eric said to the elder. "I've begun to feel haunted warnings, strange sensations I can't explain."

Thorin said nothing, yet the heavy wrinkles around his eyes tightened. He stared silently at Eric.

Eric took a deep breath and continued.

"It's as if the Norns are measuring the thread of my life, but without their murderous scissors," Eric said. "I call to the Valkyrie, ready for battle, yet I fear they don't look to me."

Thorin's brows knit, and suddenly Eric sensed danger. Jumping up, Eric kicked back his bench and retreated just as Thorin lunged at him, a long, gleaming knife in his hand.

"You dare mock me ...?" Thorin cried.

Eric dropped his hand to his swordhilt, yet he didn't draw; if he pulled a weapon then nothing would stop the fight, and he had no quarrel with Thorin.

Behind him, other elders jumped to their feet, alarmed and wary. Hands touched weapons. Yet Thorin stood glaring, and Eric offered no sign of retaliation.

"Come at me, if you dare ...!" Thorin hissed angrily. *"I'll send you to your Valkyrie ...!"*

"I didn't come to fight," Eric said, loud enough for everyone to hear. "I came for wisdom."

Thorin didn't lower his blade. Eric's frown deepened; Thorin had been a legendary warrior, a champion of jarls, when Eric had been a youth. No greater slayer could the Valkyrie have chosen to join them in sacred Valhalla, yet Thorin had never died. His fighting skills had preserved his life countless times where lesser men would've fallen. Now those times were over. Even if Thorin died tonight, gloriously, grasping a bloody sword, what maid of Odin would swoop to claim his aged, withered shell?

Anxiously Eric flexed his own wrinkled, scarred sword-hand. Eric was facing the same black fate that had etched misery across Thorin's haggard, wizened features. Surely Thorin had some advice, after all these years, and Eric's time was running short; soon he'd be too old for glory.

"If I don't die soon, I'll have nothing left to live for," Eric said grimly.

Ulftorr, one of the eldest in the hall, approached their table cautiously.

"Easy, Thorin," Ulftorr said. "Eric wasn't trying to dishonor you. He's only beginning to feel the pain we share. Pity him instead."

Eric risked looking away from Thorin's blade for an instant to cast a black stare at Ulftorr; *pity was an insult to a warrior ...!*

Thorin's blade slowly vanished into a fold of his cloak.

"I pity you, Bjornson," Thorin said cruelly.

Eric glared; no other on Earth would've dared speak so to him, yet these men were all honored slayers, dignified when he was a stripling.

"I want an answer," Eric said.

"Punish others with your complaints," Thorin growled through his heavy gray beard. "At least you still have hope."

"If we knew that answer, then none of us would be here," Ulftorr replied.

Eric looked into the elder's eyes yet saw only despair. They were once men like him, champions, too great to fall beneath the swords of lesser men. They thrived on glory ... until it became their doom.

A long silence filled the hall, yet Eric refused to accept their doom; *there had to be a way.*

"How can I gain Odin's attention?" Eric demanded, facing all the elders. "Leap into a wolf-pit ...? Challenge Svenson's whole army ...?"

"The Valkyrie look not to fools," Thorin said, his coarse voice tinged with a deep, regretful anguish.

"Speak, elder: what can I do?"

The silence in the alehouse stabbed at Eric's ears, but he waited patiently.

Finally Thorin spoke in a barest whisper:

"Make them want to kill you."

Eric paused long, carefully considering Thorin's words.

Make them want to kill me ...?

What did that mean ...?

Suddenly Ulftorr smiled, and Eric glanced at the other elders' expressions; finally he understood.

"To my last Viking!" Eric lifted his horn, and the elders raised ale-horns and cheered as much as their close-guarded dignity allowed.

Hours later, after heavy drinking, Eric sat before the fire. Even Thorin joined them, although he sat in the back, as always. Eric's upcoming death had been toasted to countless times, always followed by a toast to the Valkyrie and a prayer that all of the elders would be remembered. Finally Eric's horn was drained and he stumbled to refill it at the keg.

A fierce blast of wind burst into the alehouse. Thorland and his cohorts entered, laughing at the sodden patrons.

"Behold, men! What a sad sight! The night's barely begun, and these fool elders are already past their limit and ready for bed."

Thorland's sarcastic laughter boomed through the smoky air.

"Shut up, Thorland!" shouted someone from the corner.

"Go home, Thorland!" Ulftorr yelled. "You're not welcome here. Take your villains and get out!"

"Anyone here dare to throw out the Prince?" Thorland challenged boldly, and a long, uncomfortable silence ensued. "I thought not! Gunthar, open a new keg; you have guests of means a'waiting."

Rudely Thorland and his friends took benches at the center table, laughing and joking as the two elders they'd joined rose and went elsewhere, just as Eric stumbled back from the keg.

"Eric, you old boor!" Thorland laughed. "It's been long since your flabby shadow darkened father's court. What have you been up to of late?"

"Shut up, Thorland," Eric growled, and he walked past.

Suddenly Thorland's foot thrust between his. Eric tripped and fell, spilled his ale, and splashed atop its foamy puddle, falling hard onto his ale-horn; he heard his ancient horn crack beneath him.

Soaked with ale and snarling, Eric pushed to his feet and his fist grabbed his sword-hilt. *That had been his favorite horn!* But quickly an elder seized Eric, anxious to quell the brawl before it began.

"Let him come ...!" Thorland shouted, standing, his hand on his hilt.

Thorland's companions jumped up and kicked back their benches, eager for the fray.

Eric gritted his teeth, composed, and shook himself free.

"You think you're tough, braggart ...?" Eric tossed his empty, ruined horn onto the center of the table. "On the count of three, fast as you can, draw your sword and cut the horn in two. Ready ...?"

"What is this ...? A game ...?"

"One," Eric said.

"This is stupid."

"Two."

Thorland swallowed hard, widened his stance, and tightened his grip on his sword.

"Three."

As Thorland jerked his sword out of its silver scabbard, instantly Eric's sword seemingly leapt forward. His heavy blade swept out, arced low, and slammed onto the table right atop the ruined horn. Pieces of horn flew in all directions; Eric had severed the cracked horn before Thorland had even raised his blade.

The alehouse filled with the elder's laughter; it was an old game, almost forgotten, but still good.

A new, brimming horn was thrust into Eric's left hand with many hearty congratulations. Even Thorin laughed.

"You damn old fool ...!" Thorland cried.

The brawl struck like a winter gale. Sharp steel rang loudly over shouts and the crashes of tables overturning. Eric caught Thorland's blows against his heavier sword, but not easily. By command of his father, Thorland had been trained by the best, including Eric. Yet, between the clangs of steel, Eric's greatest desire echoed; *Do it now! Miss one block ... and die with a sword in your hand!*

No, Eric realized sadly. Eternal reward could never be earned by such a cowardly act. Nor could Eric stomach giving a fool like Thorland the satisfaction of killing him.

"Stop it, Thorland ...!" Eric warned. *"Stop now!"*

Heedless, Thorland cursed Eric and swung his bright, deadly sword ceaselessly while his companions slashed at the others. Most of the elders weren't wearing swords. Behind Thorland, Ulftorr defended himself with a bench against a huge scramsax, while Thorin grappled a knife-wielding youth one quarter his age. All had once been great warriors, yet the young fighters, though inexperienced, were strong and fast, the elders too drunk to toy with them.

Forced into a corner, Eric waited for a pause between Svenson's strikes, and then suddenly he swung hard at Thorland's sword. The clang rang loudly, and as Eric's sword rebounded, he arced it back and around at Thorland's head with blinding speed. Eric knew Thorland's only hope was ducking Eric's swing or dropping to the floor, letting Eric's blade pass overhead; Eric had taught Thorland that move. Either response would leave Thorland's face or groin exposed, and Eric's left knee into either target would end the whole affair.

Thorland failed to duck.

Eric realized it too late; his sword struck across the prince's right ear, sliced through, and penetrated deep.

Thorland fell lifeless.

Instantly the fighting ceased. A moment pregnant with dread implications hovered over the heads of all staring at the bleeding corpse: Thorland had been a bad son, unruly as a boy and cruel as a man. But he'd been a king's son.

Thorland's companions bolted out of the door and vanished into the revelry outside, shouting of

Thorland's murder. Quickly Ulftorr knelt by Thorland's still body.

"Dead," he pronounced. "Eric, go! Ride for Lappland, or steal a boat and make for the sea. Svenson won't forgive this, not ever."

"I didn't start the fight," Eric said.

"It matters not," said another. "Flee!"

"Thorland attacked me!" Eric argued. "You all witnessed ...!"

"In Odin's name, begone!" Gunthar shouted. "No Althing will you live to see! Outrun Svenson's revenge, or by his golden horn, cry for the Valkyrie and make your last stand worth a song!"

Eric glanced about at the severe, drawn faces of his oldest companions and tightened his grip on his red-dripping sword.

Thorin grinned wickedly.

"Make them want to kill you ...!"

"No!" Ulftorr cried, "Eric, run! Svenson won't allow you an honorable death! Not after this!"

"Then I'll earn one," Eric promised. "Farewell, old friends!"

"Wait not for fair partings!" Gunthar shouted, and the Alemaster threw some food and two jugs of mead into an old burlap sack, forced it into Eric's hand, and then shoved him toward the door. "Svenson'll be after you soon as he hears about this, with hundreds old like us and thousands young like Thorland. Hurry ...!"

Eric ran out into the windy night. Shouts echoed from the huge firepit surrounded by revelers. Eric flung the heavy sack over his shoulder and desperately raced towards the stables, but angry yells halted him in mid-step.

"The stables ...!" cried excited voices. *"Warn the guards to look for Eric ...!"*

Eric ran under the shadows of some thin saplings. The stables were closed to him, and he couldn't escape on foot; the sea held his last hope of escape.

Flaming torches appeared in the village, dancing as young warriors raced about. Somehow, Eric had to make it to the docks.

Darkness-cloaked from all but Valkyrie eyes, Eric darted forward, trusting the confusion to hide in. When the torches parted, Eric plunged through their gap, his sword tight in his nervous grip; death would come slowly if the youths caught him.

Cautiously Eric slipped from shadow to shadow, through the town, past aged long houses and hastily-built barracks, avoiding contact. Then, when no torches were in sight, Eric sprinted his heavy bulk up a long trail to the dunes, grimacing as each footfall noisily crunched dry, sandy weeds beneath his boots.

As he topped the last rise, Oslo Bay swayed blackly before him, the surging ocean beyond it. Eric ran low and swiftly along the edge of the tall weeds, behind driftwood and dunes, to the edge of the torchlight illuminating the guarded docks.

Eric peeked his head above the weeds and saw the village in chaos, torches flying everywhere. Boat guards were lifting lanterns and standing on rails to watch the unexpected tumult. Eric suspected that they didn't yet know of Thorland's death, or of the hunt for him, yet that wouldn't last long.

With one last deep breath, Eric rose running. He dashed across the sands, Gunthar's bag bouncing against his back. He scabbarded his sword; it would only warn the guards. Eric ran to the dock, shouting as they spied him.

"Thorland's dead …!" Eric shouted. *"The Prince is dead …!"*

Shocked faces shouted questions as Eric's boots hammered the wooden planks. Eric ran right to the end of the dock, to the farthest boat, and then suddenly he drew his sword. With one blow, Eric spliced the tether securing the ship to the dock and jumped aboard.

Too late, two shocked guards realized something was amiss. Eric charged one and bodily slammed him overboard. The other drew his sword, yet Eric was Svenson's Royal Champion; he masterfully slashed right at the joint between his opponent's blade and its hilt. Their swords clanged loudly; Eric's blow sent the smaller blade flying from the less experienced hand of the guard wielding it.

Facing Eric's naked broadsword, the guard jumped from his boat to the next. Yet other guards ran close, shouting as they leaped from deck to deck, and someone tossed him a sword.

Eric pressed his foot against the dock, trying to push the massive dragonship out into the harbor, but its weight daunted him. Other guards approached quickly, swords drawn. Eric had to withdraw his leg as they came close enough to slash at it; his dragonship had hardly budged, still within easy reach of the dock.

Seven boat guards faced Eric; three on a boat to each side, and four on the dock. Others climbed forward; soon his opponents would outnumber even his swordskills.

Eric grinned: Valhalla had to come now or he'd never see it. Eric took a deep breath, ready to berserk.

In the dark, a coarse fishing net suddenly struck Eric's face, falling over his flailing limbs. Eric struggled to flip the stout fishing net off of him before he got entangled, but his opponents jumped atop him with shouts of triumph, and seized Eric through the net. Eric struggled, but he was thrown down, a dozen men holding him, and helplessly pinned to the rocking deck.

They beat Eric's sword-hand until he was forced to release his grip, and his broadsword clattered to the deck.

Eric was disarmed ...!

They drug Eric up onto the dock, still trapped in the stout net and held by strong hands. Several torches were brought forward as men shouted the news of Eric's capture, and the whole village rushed to see. A crowd of hundreds gathered on the beach.

All parted as King Svenson Two-Sword approached.

The Norsemen cheered as Svenson walked up the long wooden dock to challenge Eric. Without a word, King Svenson Two-Sword punched his iron-hard fist straight into Eric's face.

"Eric Bjornson, you thrice-cursed, damned traitor! Tonight you die, swordless and screaming! May Hel refuse your crow-bitten spirit! Before all of my subjects you'll beg for death!" Svenson lifted his highest badge of office, his famous golden drinking horn. "To Eric's death!"

Svenson toasted, and he drank.

The crowd cheered savagely.

Eric struggled as torches dazzled his eyes, glinting off countless blades pointed at him. His heavy broadsword was gone, yet he still had his small scramsax in his hidden sheath.

Suddenly Eric threw his weight left-then-right, unbalanced his captors, and jerked his arms free. Instantly his right hand yanked out his blade, and Eric threw himself forward. The net was strong, but Eric's sharp knife quickly slashed open a small hole, and his left hand shot out and seized Svenson's heavy cloak clasp, and Eric yanked the Norse king against his chest, stabbing the point of his scramsax ungently into the king's throat under his heavy beard.

"By Odin and Asgard ...!" Eric shouted, still entangled. *"Get back! Back, you weasels, or Svenson dies now ...!"*

"Kill him ...!" many cried, but Svenson's retainers shouted them silent.

"Get back!" they ordered. *"Don't move! Weapons down!"*

"Let him go, Bjornson!"

"You can't escape!"

"Svenson will die with me, I swear ...!" Eric shouted.

Svenson's retainers ordered his army back; Eric would take Svenson to Niflhiem with him, if defied. Several complained futilely; all were warriors who, like Eric, had many times been part of war's dirtiest business, and knew Eric would kill without hesitation.

Grumbling, the Norsemen gave way, having Eric completely but ineffectually surrounded. Eric noted the hate in their eyes; most were hardened, battle-tried warriors.

"Svenson ...!" shouted one. *"What are your wishes ...?"*

"Just stay there ...!" Svenson cursed. "Eric, you bastard, let me go!"

"Go to Hel," Eric sneered at Svenson. "Your son attacked me."

"You didn't have to kill him ...!" Svenson shouted, his face twisted with grief. "He was a fool, but he was my son ...!"

"He was a Viking! Viking sons die!"

"No," Svenson growled. "No, Eric; I know you. You did this to spite me, to fatten yourself in glory like some bloated sow. You wasted your life, laughing and drinking, while I built an empire and earned my crown. Now you've ruined me. Hel looks to us; even if I live to see another son born, he won't know his father when he's grown. Thorland was to inherit all I've built so my legend would live forever. But you killed him! Damn you, Eric! *Thorland was my last hope!"*

Svenson's mighty arms flexed, his golden horn clenched in one hand as the other slid slowly towards his swordbelt, where Eric knew Svenson kept his own hidden blade.

"Don't ...!" Eric threatened. "Stop, or I'll gut you like a herring!"

The two men glared at each other in the torchlight through the weave of the net, surrounded by angry warriors.

"Give up, Eric," Svenson growled.

"Get back!" Eric shouted to the crowd. "Push us out in that dragon."

"If you kill Svenson, we'll hunt you down and torture you to death," one of Svenson's retainers promised.

"He'll live, if you obey me," Eric replied. "I just want the ship."

"We'll be close behind, no matter where you go."

"I'm counting on it."

Never releasing the pressure on his sharp scramsax stabbing into Svenson's jaw, the two warriors struggled their way down into the large, empty dragonship, encumbered by the net. Svenson glared, yet Eric watched him like a hawk; his life depended on his hostage.

"Push us off ...!" Eric ordered, and Svenson's men grudgingly obeyed; long poles pushed the craft away.

"We will send out a knarr," shouted one of the men as the dragonship slowly floated out into Oslo's darkness. "Send Svenson back to us in it."

"Not yet ...!" Eric shouted. "Wait. I'll signal you when I'm ready."

The mighty ship floated out onto the dark waters in silence.

"Eric, you'll never get away with this," Svenson promised. "If we go out any farther, they'll come after us, no matter what you do. You won't even make it out of the bay."

"I will," Eric said. "Their boat will have to stop ... to fish you out."

"Kill me instead ...!" Svenson shouted. "That water's cold ...!"

Eric pushed Svenson up against the thick mast, then flipped the net off of him, covering his king with it.

"We've both swam in colder," Eric said. "Now, turn around."

"If you're going to kill me, do it to my face," Svenson said.

"Turn around or I will kill you," Eric warned.

As Svenson obeyed, Eric slipped his knife away from his king's throat, and then ran aft. On the deck lay Eric's heavy broadsword; he scooped it up, feeling comfort in its reassuring grip.

Svenson flipped the net off of him and had his dagger out by the time Eric held his blade, yet Svenson's knife was no match for Eric's sword. Svenson scowled and sheathed his dagger.

"Thorland forced the fight," Eric said.

"I know," Svenson said. "What else can I do? If I don't kill you, then I'll be disgraced in the eyes of my men."

"You could let me fight," Eric said. "An honorable death; that's all I want."

"He was my son."

"I know."

"I can't let you escape."

"I've no desire to escape," Eric said, and he walked forward, lowered his sword, and put one hand on his king's shoulder. "Look for me atop the old foam cliffs."

"England ...? Are you sure ...?"

"We'll begin the chase at Othar."

"If I catch you, I'll boil you alive and flay the skin from your bones."

"I'll hold you to that, but I'm not easy to catch," Eric said, and he took off his warhorn and gave it to Svenson, then plucked from his hand Svenson's famous golden horn. "We have to trade horns. Recover yours when you catch me; blow mine to summon your men, to keep them from sailing past you in the dark. I'll keep your horn with me; it'd do you little good if it sinks to the bottom of the bay."

Svenson frowned. "Keep it safe."

"I will," Eric said. "Farewell, old friend."

"Farewell, Eric," Svenson said.

Svenson stepped up to the rail, glanced one last time at Eric, and then raised Eric's warhorn to his lips. Svenson blew a loud, mighty blare, trumpeting to his men, and jumped overboard.

The cold ocean waters splashed loudly, and shouts of vengeance came from the docks. Eric ignored them, grabbed the mast-line, pulled up the heavy sail, and then fell upon the stout rudder and steered for his life.

Eric grinned as the strong north wind puffed out the striped sail. His mighty dragonship lurched forward, gaining speed. Svenson and his men would soon be pursuing him in all their ocean-worthy ships, twenty fully-manned dragonships, and scores of lesser crafts, minutes after Svenson was rescued.

Eric had only one advantage: though he couldn't man the thirty oars, his craft was unburdened with men. He'd skim lighter over the waves. If the winds kept blowing south, then Eric could outsail them all.

Eric lifted up Svenson's golden horn with a sly grin. With this, played right, Eric could buy, barter, or betray for his life, his death, or anything else he wanted.

A devious plan formed in his mind, and Eric settled himself against the tiller, in the rear of the mighty dragonship, and steered through the driving surf, out of the mouth of Oslo Bay, and straight toward England.

* * * * * * * * * * *

Eric's memories offered little comfort as he walked, his ghostly form pacing step by step over the black North Sea. Even his phantom right arm ended at the elbow where Svenson had hacked it off. It'd been Svenson's final revenge, denying Eric his rightful place in Valhalla; Svenson's blackest deed.

Utter hopelessness shrouded Eric's soul. *His friends hadn't forsaken him;* he clung to that tiny hope with every ounce of his spirit-form. Whatever they hoped to accomplish, Eric could only do as they'd asked ... and pray that they succeeded.

Chapter 14

Sweet Sailing

THE SEER

No glowing 'V's appeared on the black starlit waters.

Dejected, the Seer crawled inside the canopy. He was shivering; even his thick cloak couldn't keep out the dawn's sea-cold as they sailed northeast under the waning moon. He had no idea where they were; without a map, their compass and sextant were useless. Worse, the Seer had no idea where Eric was.

Inside the awning, cut off from the wind, the others lay asleep, but it was too dark to see. Hands trembling, the Seer reached into his robe and pulled out a tiny candle. He closed his eyes and concentrated:

The Lady is his light, his spark, the fire of his spirit, the heat that burns deep inside him, the raging inferno of his ambition ...!

The candle lit, brightening their tented fore. The Seer felt the expected twinge, as if a tiny light within him had died forever, as if he'd reached inside his soul to draw part of his own light into reality, leaving his soul lessened.

The Seer frowned; Karl lay snuggled against Eloise's back, and she had her arms wrapped around Roselyn. The Seer didn't know why Roselyn had seduced him while they were drunk, a state he normally never allowed; drunkenness was a poisoning of mind and body. He didn't like losing control, especially not before others. But he'd been tired, mourning, and ... out of sorts. His usual evenings were spent in solitude, reading, dining alone, and trying out small experiments, most of which never worked. Since meeting with these insane companions, the Seer had experienced magics of levels he'd seldom risked before ... not since his studies on the Isle. The Lady's errand had gotten him out of his house and tested his abilities like never before.

It had felt good to sit with fairies again. He'd summoned fairies before, as had all masters of Druid lore; it was part of their training. He'd once amazed all of his teachers and fellow students by calling forth a dozen beautiful fairies at once, which danced and sang before them. Yet he'd never seen Titania or hundreds of her folk at a Fairie well.

He'd never before faced a giant, especially not an illusion-caster. He'd never commanded such powerful illusions and had credited the old credo: *Magic begets magic;* being near the magical giant, he must've siphoned off some of his energy, and their combined magics had helped both of their spell castings.

Finding out that Eloise bore the wolf-curse had given the Seer a rare chance to study, and then to meet Eric's ghost, three weeks dead, and follow his tracks across the sea; the Lady must be stirring his life with Her own finger to cause so much wild magic.

Yet all of that seemed to pale beside the memory of Roselyn holding him tightly.

No ...! He had to stay in control. He was disciplined, self-mastered, and decisive. He had to be: everything he was, all he'd ever attained, he attributed to superior mental skills, enhanced by Druid training on the Enchanted Isle, and endless hours of practice every day. He couldn't afford to be consumed by lust or jealousy; he was on a mission for the Lady Herself.

Women weren't new to him. Many lived on the Isle, and several priestesses had attracted his eyes to the point of distraction, but he was young then, too eager to indulge in ancient secrets than to let women interfere. Since the Isle, he'd comforted himself once or twice in the brothels, but it served him little; he wanted more than the touch of a strange woman. The Seer wanted to be accepted, and for one night in Castle Bristlen, he'd thought he was.

Cold tingles stabbed. He could use his magic to warm himself, but he felt so depressed that, if he drew any more light out of his spirit, it might grow dark forever; he had to get under the blankets. Quietly the Seer crouched low, so he didn't touch the damp awning and start it dripping, crawled to the far side, and slid under an edge of a wool blanket beside Seren, where he gently spread his wool cloak over her. There had been room for him next to Roselyn, yet he didn't think he could handle that. The Seer blew out his candle, waited until its wax solidified, and then slid it back in its pocket. Lying on his back, barely covered by blanket and cloak, he laid awake long, staring at the darkness.

Seren was the only one still sleeping when he awoke; she'd flung one arm over him, clinging tightly for warmth. The Seer slowly sat up, and Seren stirred and groaned.

"Seren ...?"

"Stomach ...!"

"Sea sickness," he said. "Lay still. I'll examine you."

The Seer felt her forehead, pressed his ear against her chest and stomach, and stretched back her eyelids to reveal deep red lines.

"I've some herbs that should help," the Seer said. "I'll make tea."

The Seer crawled out onto the deck. The sky was thick with tall white clouds in and over a sea of blue. The sun was bright, peeking between white billows.

"Seren's seasick," the Seer said. "Chamomile tea will soothe her. I've a small amount."

"We have lots of chamomile in the Viking's gear," Eloise said.

"She needs hot tea," the Seer said.

"I'll start the fire," Karl said. "Rafe, we'll have to move the awning."

"I'll unlash it," Rafe said.

"I'll get our canteens," Eloise said.

They all got started. Left alone, the Seer looked at Roselyn, and she looked like a deer in the torchlight. Giving her no time, he sat down beside her.

"Are you sorry ...?" the Seer asked.

Roselyn swallowed hard. She drew in a deep breath ... and the Seer's heart caved, expecting the customary *'like a brother'* speech.

"Roselyn ...?" Eloise called. "Where's that large cooking pot?"

The Seer's eyes met Roselyn's. She faced him squarely, neither defiant nor demure, and suddenly she stood up, leaned over, and kissed him on his forehead, and then she hurried to help Eloise.

The Seer sat flabbergasted, frustrated. Roselyn had purposely sent him a mixed signal; she was trying to confuse and delay him. The Seer sighed and stared at her as she knelt to help Eloise; *did she really expect him to be fooled by childish love-games?*

Strong winds whipped his black hair into his eyes and he didn't even blink.

Finally remembering, the Seer reached into his black pouch and pulled out his moonstone. He held it up so its invisible light shined on both sides of the stern. Nothing: not one glowing 'V' floated on the water.

Rafe shortened the awning past the firepit, yet not all the way; Roselyn insisted that they needed some place for privacy. Over one ear of the carven dragonhead, Roselyn had hung a wooden bucket with a short rope tied to it, so the women could have a privy: they could throw the fouled bucket over the bow for a minute and the sea would wash it clean.

When finished, Rafe and Karl came back and sat aft while the women boiled tea.

"The wind's picking up," Rafe said. "It'll blow hard tonight. We should make good time if we tack northwest this afternoon, then northeast tonight."

"It doesn't matter," the Seer said. "I've no idea where Eric is."

"Karl and I have been talking about that," Rafe said. "In this wind, this vessel is traveling fast, more miles per day than any man could walk. Perhaps we passed Eric already. If he were walking across the waves, one step at a time, then he'll be days reaching here."

"These aren't safe waters," Karl said. "Vikings sail here, as do Danes, Scots, and the Irish; we'd be hard-pressed to resist any of them, if they boarded us. Vikings aren't the only pirates."

"So we have another dilemma," the Seer said.

"Two more," Rafe said. "We didn't leave Demril quietly; Sir Guldwin will hear of our passage soon enough. He won't tolerate others to know we escaped and do nothing; he'll send ships after us, or messengers to every port to announce the prices on our heads."

"Damned if we go, damned if we wait," the Seer said.

"Sums it up," Karl said.

"We need to locate Eric," Rafe said.

"I know that!" the Seer snapped. "I just don't know how, not without risking even greater danger. The only spell that could help might kill me, and without me, what chance would the Lady's quest have?"

Karl and Rafe exchanged glances.

"How do you know what the Lady's quest is?" Rafe asked. "Maybe you've already accomplished it."

"Maybe she just wanted you on this ship," Rafe said. "If so, then your quest is finished."

"I'll know when Her will is finished," the Seer said. "Until then, I have to stay on the road She placed before me. But you talk as if you're ready to quit. What of your quest for Eric's soul? For Eloise's cure?"

"We've seen a lot of strange things, Seer," Karl said.

"Enough to no longer doubt any tale or legend entirely," Rafe added.

"... but to go where you're suggesting; doesn't it sound like certain death?" Karl asked. "We know nothing of this 'crack in the world'. Maybe it doesn't exist, or it's death to pass through it. We have this ship, and the world's wide. We can sail anywhere, do anything ...!"

"Have you asked the women?" the Seer sneered.

Rafe and Karl looked guilty.

"I thought not. Convince them to give up on Eric, if you can. Besides, Eloise hopes to find a cure for her curse, and none exists in this world. What will she say to your plan? Will you abandon her as well?"

"No one said anything about abandoning!" Rafe said. "But we want proof that this 'crack' isn't just someone's imagination."

"Just imagination ...?" the Seer chuckled. "But imagination is everything, the key to intelligence; all Druids know this. To animals, to nature, there're no falsehoods. Animals may deceive each other for food, but they can't grasp concepts like lies. What is ... simply is, and what isn't is never considered. Only in the minds of humans do falsehoods exist. They're the core of human intelligence: by seeing falsehoods, humans compare, think, and reason. We elevate our minds with imaginings; new ideas and possibilities. Lies allow us to see truths. Animals don't see truths because truths don't exist without falsehoods.

"Titania verified that there was a 'crack'. The only proof I can give you, beyond her word, is to take you there and show you; that's what I am doing."

Karl and Rafe bowed their heads. The Seer kept his expression blank, yet inside he was annoyed; these were simple men of the land: *idiots.* All he ever wanted was a few friends of his own intelligence, and he was surrounded by peasants who never used an ounce more of their brains than absolutely necessary.

Hours later, Eloise fussed.

"I hate sailing!" she scowled.

"Why ...?" Karl asked.

"Because there's nothing to do!"

"Real sailors never just sit," Rafe said. "I suspect there's plenty to do. We're doing nothing because we don't know what needs to be done."

"How do we learn?" Eloise asked.

"Let's hope we don't," Rafe said. "By the time we discover it, we'll be in trouble."

"Well, I'm enjoying it," Roselyn said, leaning back and relaxing.

"Seer, what kind of magic is safe to do?" Eloise asked. "You must know some."

"What do you want?" the Seer asked.

"I don't care," Eloise said.

The Seer slowly smiled. He reached inside his robe and pulled out a tiny gold chain with a plain golden cross hanging from it.

"You look relaxed, Countess," the Seer said to Roselyn. "I might be able to show you some real magic, if you'd volunteer."

"What do I have to do?" Roselyn asked.

"Just relax, keep your head still, and let you're your eyes follow my cross as it swings back and forth," the Seer dangled his cross close before her eyes. "Relax. Let yourself drift. Just watch the cross."

The Seer swung his cross back and forth. Roselyn watched, but as the Seer repeated the same slow, soft words, over and over again, she quickly fell asleep. Eloise didn't look impressed.

The Seer hesitated: he could ask Roselyn personal questions, but not in front of the others; he was too afraid of what her answers might be.

"You're a chicken," the Seer said. "Cluck like a chicken."

Roselyn obeyed, and the companions laughed and laughed. Then the Seer made her snort like a pig and sing like a canary. Eloise rolled onto her side against the sides, clutching her ribs, and Karl almost fell overboard in hysterics.

Roselyn denied everything when the Seer woke her. Arguments infuriated; Roselyn glared at the Seer as if to burn holes through him. The Seer tried to apologize, yet he couldn't keep from smiling, so she refused to forgive him.

At first, the Seer felt injured. They were using his hard-learned skills for amusement, to while away hours. Yet the effort was small. He joined in their revelry, and the others displayed no sign he wasn't welcome. Seren even complemented him several times, especially on his herb-lore, which had eased her queasiness.

He wanted to hate these people. His father was dead because of them. The men of Grusshire had never refused to flee before invading Vikings arrived. Yet he felt ... almost accepted, more welcome than he'd ever felt in Madrone.

"Can you read my palm?" Eloise asked.

"I can tell interpret your lines, if that's what you want," the Seer said. "Yet I don't claim it's real. Most palm-readers tell nothing but lies. I've done it before, for reward, but I've never studied it deeply."

"Read my palm," Eloise insisted, holding out her right hand.

"Start with the left hand," the Seer said. "The right shows the present, the left the past."

"Yes, let's hear Eloise's secrets," Seren grinned.

"Wait," Eloise said, looking at the others, leaning forward to listen. "Let's go under the canopy; I want to hear my secrets before I decide if I want everyone to know them."

Everyone complained, demanding to listen, but the Seer grudgingly got up and followed Eloise. The sea was calm, the winds slow, so the deck was only tilting slightly. He crawled inside the canopy behind her.

Eloise pulled the hanging flap closed, and then waited a few seconds, and shouted at the others straining to listen. Their shadows, which had grown on the canopy, slid away. Finally she held out her left hand.

The Seer balanced, struggled to sit, and then took her hand gently.

Despite their difficulties, Eloise's hands were surprisingly supple. There were a few fading blisters, probably from digging the grave in Grusshire, but no calluses, not even on the fingers where seamstresses got tiny scars; any fortune-teller would know she'd never done any hard work. Her lines were all normal with a few exceptions; her lifeline crossed her fate line deep near the wrist, and the four major lines made a jagged 'M' upon her palm. Traditionally that was the sign that the course of her life would be decided early, and that she had an affinity for magic. Eloise had three children lines under her pinky, two dark; those would be her sons. Yet Eloise wanted to hear lies, so the Seer began making some up.

"You're lying to me," Eloise finally interrupted him.

"I told you I would," he said.

"I want the truth."

"What do you want to know?"

"Why did you sleep with Roselyn?"

The Seer froze. Eloise laughed.

"Roselyn's right," Eloise said. "We're really, finally free. Out here, on this boat, we don't have to be what royal courts decree. We can act like men, or women, however we feel. No one will judge us, and we can be ourselves."

"You don't want your palm read ...?"

"No."

Eloise traced her finger up the sleeve of his black robe. The Seer's inner warnings alarmed; he should resist, not be weak, yet he didn't want to. Eloise was right: onboard, they didn't have to conform to society's morals. Even the Druid Council couldn't call him to task for what he did aboard this ship.

Women weren't the only ones with rigid expectations. The Seer had lived his whole life being excluded, even by his fellow Druids. He wondered what it'd be like to be really free, uninhibited, yet he remained suspicious.

"Why ...?"

"Do I need a reason ...?"

Eloise leaned forward and kissed him.

"Eventually I'll have to go back, and become Baroness, and then I'll lose this freedom; I don't want to waste it."

"Druid women don't lose freedom."

"I'm no Druid," Eloise said. "I'm a Saxon, your baroness, and I'll have what I please."

She started unbuttoning his robe. The Seer made no move to stop her. Perhaps she only wanted him because he'd slept with Roselyn, or perhaps she simply wanted to explore her newfound freedom to its limits. He should object; he was a Druid Seer, not her plaything. Yet, as her teeth sank lightly into his neck, the Seer knew she could toy with him forever and he'd only ask for more.

Eloise and the Seer rejoined the others an hour later, the Seer biting his tongue to keep from blushing; they hadn't been quiet. Eloise smiled brightly, triumphantly, and Roselyn surprised the Seer by smiling at him. He felt his cheeks redden and turned to face the sea so the others couldn't see.

Rafe adjusted the sails, and then he and Seren vanished inside the awning; the Seer tried not to notice. Karl was teaching Roselyn how to hold the tiller, which they'd untied, and their boat splashed across the waves faster.

"If you hold it just right then it really flies!" Karl said. "We should've been doing this all along."

The Seer grinned, yet inside he was heartbroken. They'd lost Eric's trail, and going faster wouldn't find him. Yet he felt strangely light, as if a new light illuminated his soul. Eloise absently clutched his arm to keep from falling, while she stood to let the wind blow upon her.

He'd missed human contact for too long. In Madrone, few would stand near him, and no one touched him. He'd learned to live apart ... and wrongly considered it a blessing.

The Seer feared his feelings. He had no idea what the Lady's plans were. He doubted if She cared whether Eric's spirit was restored to Valhalla; what was he but another Viking savage? Her needs required this road, but what would he do when he'd satisfied Her quest? Eric had already been sacrificed to fulfill Her plans. Human sacrifice wasn't unknown to Druids.

What if the Seer developed feelings for these people, and Her needs required him to sacrifice them?

The Seer held Eloise tightly as she balanced on the deck. He wouldn't let go, not ever, unless She ordered him to.

Eventually Rafe and Seren crawled out, grinning widely. Karl and Roselyn disappeared under the canopy shortly after. The Seer bit back a chuckle, wondering if they should name their ship The Flying Brothel. Yet he wasn't jealous or anxious; for the first time in years, he was being included instead of being shunned.

It felt ... *good.*

The Seer took his turn at the tiller, feeling the ship bend and flex as he steered it. The ship was a simple device, yet gave off a feeling similar to magic: the power to catch the wind just right, to feel the ship lurch faster under control, was addictive. Too soon Eloise insisted on steering, so he let her master the winds while he studied the rigging.

As the sun sank, Rafe stretched the awning out again, lashing it on both sides of their ship before darkness fell. He didn't go under the canvas; they could all hear Karl and Roselyn laughing from inside the canopy. Yet soon they heard a snap-slapping, and saw the sunken canopy rise; someone was inserting the horizontal wooden slats that supported the canvas from underneath.

"We need a fire in there ... or its cold supper," Rafe shouted.

"There's a fire in ... *ouch!"* Karl shouted, and everybody laughed.

After a hearty meal, the Seer took a candle lantern and went out to man the tiller. He turned the sails first so they'd tack straight west to watch for Eric's tracks. Steering manually, he could cover much more ground than he could otherwise. The Seer held the tiller firmly, feeling their dragon skim over the ocean, and occasionally held his moonstone high, looking for signs of Eric.

The temperature sank as the stars came out, yet he set his glass-enclosed lantern firmly between his boots and let the lantern warm him from inside his thick robe and cloak. He struggled to concentrate, but found it difficult; he was just too happy.

Chapter 15

Storms at Sea

RAFE

Rafe crawled out from under the canopy to a grim dawn; dark clouds obscured a red, angry-rising sun. He frowned to see it.

Red sky at night, sailor's delight.

Red sky in the morning, sailor's warning.

A moist, heady wind blew strongly across their deck, and seagulls filled the sky. The seagull's cries squawked strangely, warning of urgency.

Only one thing drew seagulls far out to open sea: *a storm was brewing!*

Rafe tried to recall all the sailor-stories he knew; tales told by men who knew ships and understood the sea. Rafe searched their tales for pearls of wisdom and clues; anything that might help. What they needed was experience ... or they were going to sink.

If only they had a map! He knew how to use a compass, and the Seer had shown him how Farmer Tiller's sextant worked, but without a map they were useless. They should head for the closest land to wait out the storm, but in which direction was land? Seagulls would fly toward land when the storm approached, yet that would happen too late; the storm would be upon them.

Land was dangerous, since they'd never docked a ship, yet a violent sea was the greatest danger of all. Stories told by washed-up sailors were terrifying, how waves as big as Othar had crushed their ships and killed most of their crew. If the coming storm had any teeth, it'd bite them in half.

No sense telling the others about it, Rafe thought. He'd make all preparations, lash everything down, and tell them the storm only it if it hit.

Something else was wrong: the ship was leaning to starboard, not sailing fast. Rafe walked aft.

"Seer ...?" Rafe asked.

The magician was asleep. Leaned back against the wooden tail, the Seer's head rested on his shoulder, mouth open, one arm slumped over the tiller. Rafe grinned and shook his head.

"Up ...!" Rafe said, and he pulled him to groggily stand and pushed him toward the awning. "Go sleep under blankets. I'll handle it."

The Seer mumbled something inaudible, lost in the wind, and staggered toward the canvas shelter.

Rafe glanced aft at the rising sun; they were headed west. Manning the tiller, he slowly turned their ship around, then adjusted the lines. West was open sea, all the way to the brink, which fishermen called Sailor's Doom. Directly east wasn't the direction he wanted either; the closest land would be Sweden, if they were farther north, or Denmark, if they were farther south. Neither held much hope, for they could scarcely make either shore before nightfall.

Rafe checked his compass and headed northeast. The sea would kill them little quicker than Earl Sir Guldwin, and it was possible they'd spy other boats, if they got close enough to land. Vikings were less hospitable than Saxons, but also less likely to have heard of the price on their heads. If Rafe spotted another sail then he'd follow it, assuming its captain knew what he was doing.

Rafe released another mast line to tighten it; the strong wind tilted the ship, and the sail almost pulled the rigging from his hands. Rafe held tight to the rope, surprised when it the wind lifted him off of his feet.

"Karl ...!" Rafe cried.

Boots against the rail, Rafe struggled to keep from being flung overboard. Rafe pulled hard, straining muscles he'd forgotten he had. Karl stuck his head out of the flap, then ran to help. Together they dragged the line back and secured it to its tie-down.

Minutes later, the sail billowed to its maximum, Rafe leaned back against the tiller, trying to calm his nerves. He'd been lucky; much thinner, Karl would've been tossed overboard.

Karl sat beside him on the rail, holding on as the ship bounced, looking up at the sky.

"Storm coming," Karl said.

Rafe grinned: *so much for keeping it secret.* He untied the tiller and manned it, pressing for every ounce of speed. Strong winds were their only hope; perhaps they'd get pushed to safety in time.

"We're in trouble," Rafe admitted. "If we toss everything we don't need overboard, we'd lighten our ship and travel faster. Yet I recall hearing sailors talking about ballast, the weight of their ship keeping it from capsizing."

"We're going to die if we get caught out here in a storm," Karl said. "If we lighten the load, perhaps we'll sail out of it."

"Perhaps," Rafe said, "or ... it'd be foolish to lose our ballast if we know we're going to get caught."

"We'll sink in a storm, ballast or no," Karl said.

"Very well," Rafe shook his head. "God help us."

"I'll toss while you steer," Karl said, and he began pulling up deck planks.

Heavy wooden oars went first. One by one, Karl heaved them into the water, as far from the boat as he could. Karl piled the extra rope next to Rafe; they wouldn't need all of it and could toss the worst. He kept a few extra swords, but tossed a dozen spears and axes into the ocean.

Roselyn and Eloise came out. Eloise looked up, examining the sky.

"Storm coming," Eloise said. "Why are you ...?"

"Lightening the load," Karl said. "Everything we don't need goes."

"Are we in trouble?" Roselyn asked.

"Inexperienced sailors are always in trouble," Karl replied. "Hey, there's an anvil down here."

"Toss it over," Rafe said.

"Why would anyone bring an anvil on a ship?"

"To repair the ship if it breaks," Rafe said. "There should be all sorts of tools aboard. Keep an axe, a saw, and one hammer. Dump the rest."

Rafe leaned hard on the tiller and squeezed for speed. He'd spent too much time protecting these youngsters to let them drown.

Karl spent two hours sorting and tossing unneeded supplies into the sea, even their spare weapons and armor from Bristlen, saving only their mail, helms, and Roselyn's armor. Karl tied both their swords to a large chest, and stored their shields on the very bottom. Then he lashed down everything he could before he slipped the deck planks back into place.

"That takes care of the aft section," Karl said. "What about the fore?"

"Got to do it," Rafe said. "Wake Seren and the Seer. That storm's coming fast."

Three hours later, they were securely battened down. They kept all of their food and water, and their gear, but got rid of everything else, except their saddles.

Rafe let Roselyn steer while he unlaced their awning, taking it off completely.

"Won't we need it?" Roselyn asked.

"Badly," Rafe said, "but we'll have to drop the sail when the storm hits, and we can't do that while the awning's up."

"What if it starts to rain before then?" Eloise asked.

"Then we get wet."

The sun came out around noon, and everyone relaxed, thinking their arduous preparations had been in vain. Then dark clouds swarmed overhead and rain poured in buckets. Waves grew wilder, such that they crashed through them, jolting and shaking their dragon.

Seren and Eloise passed out cloaks, yet the wind only tore at their flapping edges, and they had to hold them closed. Rafe tied ropes across the deck from rail to rail, crisscrossing the aft like a spider's web, from the mast to the tail.

"These are to hold on to, to keep from being swept overboard," Rafe said.

He hoped they wouldn't be needed. He'd heard about sailors tying themselves down, yet was hesitant to suggest it; he didn't want them drowning because they were bound to the ship.

Vengefully the full force of the storm struck. Winds blasted; Eloise's cloak flew like a kite and pulled her to the rail, threatening to drag her overboard. Seren grabbed and drug her down, onto the deck.

Rafe left the Seer to steer and called for Karl to help him at the mast. Together they lowered the heavy sail; the fighting winds flapped wet canvas madly, even after it was mostly atop lashed ropes and pinned under the boom. While Karl struggled to hold it down, Rafe reset the lifelines overtop the boom, and started lacing the awning back over the fore as the rain drenched them all. Roselyn helped, and Rafe finally managed to tie it to both sides, and Seren and Eloise crawled underneath and pushed up the thin slats in place to hold the awning up. After a brief discussion, Rafe laced the rest of the awning over the aft, leaving only a small section open so they could man the tiller.

When finished, Rafe forced the Seer inside and took the helm himself. Waves crashed over rails onto the canvas, and sometimes the whole ship heaved upwards, then dropped suddenly. Afraid of being catapulted, Rafe tied a stout loop of rope around his chest and the wooden tail. Screams of the others rose from under the awning every time they dropped, yet he stayed where he was.

'Captain Sir Rafe' he scoffed; the most inexperienced sailor knew more than he did, and would probably be less afraid. As they crashed down into deep troughs, the towering, foamy waves terrified him. It was mid-afternoon, yet the sky was black.

The dragon tilted hard. One rail went under. Rafe screamed, yet the ship righted, the naked mast swinging back and forth as it rocked. Rafe tried to steer away from the biggest waves, not knowing if that was wise, but to little avail. The deadly waves were too many, too unpredictable, coming from every side.

Rafe steeled himself; they'd survived worse than bad weather, and he wasn't going to let a little storm end his life. He didn't have any treasure left, no jewels, no comfortable retirement he'd spent his life earning. He was homeless, a wanted man with a price on his head, hated and pursued by the most powerful Noble in Northumbria. He was on a mad quest and could die at any moment. Yet he had Seren. He had Roselyn, Eloise, and Karl; Rafe had never been so rich.

He had too much to live for to drown. He held tight, and fought the tiller, which constantly wrenched away from him, and then slammed into his stomach, pushed by the waves.

The storm grew worse. Cold sheets of rain blinded. Waves of foam cascaded over their awning, often burying the whole ship in gray bubbles. Salt stung his eyes, and the chill wind's roar stabbed his ears, deafened by echoing crashes of waves.

Their ship hurled skyward, then was thrown like a spear into a mountain of water. The dragonhead vanished into the sea, and the ocean rose to consume him. Rafe gasped a last breath, and then saltwater struck his face.

An eternity Rafe foundered, underwater, his whole universe fear, salt, and foam. Then it fell away; Rafe gasped for breath. The wave that had swallowed their ship had fallen; their boat had resurfaced, yet the waves looked even bigger.

A huge wave crashed upon their port. Rafe held his breath and prayed. He couldn't see or hear, and despaired of surviving. When it washed away, their awning had collapsed; their deck flooded with pools of seawater. Aft, the wet canvas hung flat upon the low ropes, except for around the mast, where he could see outlines of his companions huddled around the base of their only sturdy beam.

The wooden slats must've broken. Rafe wondered how long it'd be before their whole ship splintered and dropped them into the frothing North Sea.

Rafe spied movement; someone was crawling toward him under the canvas upheld by ropes.

Suddenly water splashed up from his feet. Rafe looked as best he could; it splashed again ... from under the deck planks. Their dragon was filling with water; if this kept up, no matter how he steered, they'd eventually sink.

Rafe reached for the canvas and lifted it up as the figure crawled closer. The Seer, crawling on his belly across the deck, stuck his head out. His expression was panicked, terrified.

"What're you doing?" Rafe shouted.

"Saving us!" the Seer cried. "Get under here with me!"

"What ...?"

"Do it!"

Rafe looked at the sea in all its fury as a bolt of lightning illuminated a sailor's Hell; he was failing. The Seer could do no better, but he had magic, so he was their only hope.

As the ship lurched and fell, Rafe untied himself from the rope around his chest, holding onto the Seer's arm as he did, then hurled himself across the pitching deck. He crawled under the fallen canvas.

"Take care of my body!" the Seer shouted into his ear. *"I may appear dead, but I won't be!"*

Rafe knelt beside him, wondering what he was talking about, yet the Seer pushed out from under the canvas. Dragging his cloak in one hand, the Seer dangerously tried to stand on the rocking deck.

"Are you crazy ...?" Rafe shouted, but the Seer ignored him.

"Eric ...!" the Seer shouted, looking up at the dark, lightning-flashing sky. *"Only you can save us! Link with me now ... or you'll never see Valhalla!"*

Waves crashed, wind howled, and the shift lifted and fell, buffeted from both sides, yet the Seer stood alone, almost unmoving, save with the rocking of the ship. Then the Seer flung up his cloak, and threw it down onto the drenched deck. He shouted arcane words, then screamed a horrible death-knell, impudent against the fury of the storm.

Suddenly his scream cut off. Rafe grabbed the Seer's ankles, holding tight to keep him from being swept away, and the Seer collapsed on top of him, falling onto the deck atop the soaked canvas.

Rafe pushed out of the canvas. The Seer lay unconscious, limp, flailing back and forth as the ship pitched. Rafe pulled, trying to drag him back under the canvas.

Then a terrible sight froze him.

Upon the deck, Seer's empty cloak inflated. Slowly it rose off of the wet boards, and swelled until it stood alone, empty, yet shaped like a grown man stood inside it. Fierce winds buffeted it, yet the cloak resisted.

One fold of the empty cloak reached out, and wrapped a layer of black cloth around a wet line of the rigging, and another black fold slid around the flailing arm of the tiller. It seized the tiller and held it firm. The winds tore at it, yet the empty cloak stood, buffeted but resisting, as if a mighty man were wearing it, although no feet stood beneath it.

"Eric ....!" Rafe shouted.

The empty cloak ignored him, yet pushed on the tiller and pulled on the rope. Another wave crashed onto the deck, drenching them both, yet the invisible figure in the cloak heeded it not at all.

Rafe gathered his wits and dragged the Seer back under the canvas. The floating cloak stayed where it was, steering their ship and fighting the storm.

Rafe crossed himself, then pulled the canvas completely over him. Whether or not it was Eric, there wasn't anything Rafe could do about it. If it was Eric, then Rafe had to trust him: Eric alone had the nautical skills to sail in a storm.

By his robe, Rafe drug the unconscious Seer as he crawled under the wet, fallen canopy, toward the mast where the others huddled, clinging for safety. A heavy wave smashed Rafe flat, and then water splashed his face from below, yet Rafe kept crawling.

Except for the frequent flashes of lightning, it was too dark to see, but Eloise screamed when Rafe put his hand on her leg.

"It's me ...!" Rafe shouted, and he pulled the Seer up with him, when a flash of lightning illuminated their collapsed, wet canvas. They'd tied a loop of rope around them all, their backs to the mast, and were holding up the wet canvas with their hands.

"What about the rudder ...?" Karl shouted.

"Forget it ...!" Rafe shouted back, not trying to explain. *"The boat's filling with water! We have to start bailing!"*

"What happened ...?" Roselyn shouted, looking at the Seer.

"Just hold him ...!" Rafe shouted back, and he crawled past them, over their legs and headed for the front of the ship. "Karl, come!"

Another wave flattened him, yet he couldn't stop. Rafe pushed to the fore, found the lacings of the awning, and began untying them in the dark. Karl crawled up behind him just as he opened the awning. Rafe held on to the rail and lifted up several deck planks; a huge deluge of water splashed up.

"Where's that bucket ...?" Rafe shouted.

They took turns bailing, one heavy bucket-full at a time, out of the hull and over the rail. Waves smashed both down and undid their efforts. The deck was also filling with water, deep pools gathered on the canvas, which surged towards them when the nose of the ship dropped.

Karl grabbed the edge of the canvas and held it up, directing the deck-water over the side as it rushed at them. Rafe kept bailing.

In a flash of lightning, Karl spied the cloaked figure standing aft, manning the tiller. He glanced questioningly at Rafe, but Rafe only shook his head.

"Something the Seer did ...!" Rafe shouted. *"Ignore it ... and keep bailing!"*

Chapter 16

Of Sails and Secrets

KARL

The mournful cry of a seagull announced the dawn.

Karl awoke shivering, soaking wet, buried in heavy canvas. He pushed it up, and heard the women groan; they were still tied to the mast. Rafe lay beside him, sleeping. The Seer lay near the women, also unconscious.

Their ship wasn't rocking violently, just slowly swaying.

"We did it ...!" Karl shouted. *"The storm's over ... and we're alive!"*

Quickly Karl untied the laces near the mast and pushed out from under the wet canvas. Blue sky stretched overhead, clouds white and high floating peacefully, and the sea was calm.

Karl spied the cloaked figure still holding the tiller. Hesitantly, Karl walked aft across the slippery canvas, still holding pools of seawater. He grabbed the rail to steady him as he stepped across the fallen ropes Rafe had strung.

"Who are you ...?" Karl demanded.

The hooded figure said nothing.

"Answer me ...!" Karl shouted.

Receiving not even a gesture of reply, Karl grew angry. Karl seized the figure and tried to shake it, only to scream and pull back; the black cloak of the hooded figure was ice-cold, frozen, and didn't even move when he grabbed it.

"Karl ...!" Rafe shouted. *"Get away from that ...!"*

Ignoring Rafe's warning, Karl slowly lifted one finger, reached out to the concealing hood, and lifted up its chilled edge. Inside the concealing hood, Karl saw ... the inside back of the hood, with nothing but emptiness holding it up.

Karl screamed and jumped back, slipped upon Rafe's ropes, and fell, splashing onto the deck. Frantically flailing and kicking, Karl suddenly felt strong hands grab him.

"Karl, stop ...!" Rafe shouted. *"The Seer did it! It's Eric ...!"*

Karl paused, disbelieving, as the women crowded close.

"Eric ...?" Karl gasped.

"I watched him do it," Rafe said. "He knew Eric was a sailor, and that only he could save us. He cast a spell, bringing this ... thing ... here."

"Eric in cloak ...?" Seren asked.

"I don't know," Rafe said. "The Seer implied he would be, but he passed out when this thing arose. He'd just called upon Eric, but I don't know; maybe his spell didn't work right. But this thing saved us from the storm. I think we should leave it be until the Seer awakens."

Karl looked back at the empty cloak, hovering in the broad sunlight as if a tall, broad-shouldered man stood under it, and wondered if it were Eric.

"Moonstone ...?" Seren asked.

"Yes, the moonstone will show us," Karl agreed.

"So, you're becoming a wizard now ...?" Rafe laughed, his humor startling in the morning. "Farmer, guard, and now a seer ...?"

Karl scowled; *the very idea was sickening.*

"We'll wait until the Seer wakes up," Karl growled.

"Where are we?" Roselyn asked.

"Lost, I suspect," Rafe said, standing up and looking across the empty sea. "Well, we'd better start cleaning up, try to dry out our things, and see if there's any damage."

They pulled up a few deck planks to find the hull still deep with water. Karl found their bucket floating overboard, still tied to their ship; he hauled it in and bailed while the others started to work.

Eventually the water level in the hull dropped noticeably, yet everything was soaked, including all their food. The baskets of breads and grain were ruined, and turnips and onions floated in bilge water.

Rafe strung several lines across the ship, from dragonhead to mast, and shrugged.

"Here we go again," he said, and he began unbuttoning his clothes.

Karl was shivering, yet not as badly as the women. They were all as soaked as if they'd been swimming. They couldn't start a fire because their meager supply of wood was sodden; again, they had no choice.

Minutes later, all undressed, ringing out their wet clothes over the rail, and hanging them on the lines Rafe had strung. Rafe undressed the Seer from his wet robe, which he hung near the dragon-head. Yet the Seer remained unconscious.

The sun quickly dried and warmed their skin, and their shivering ceased. Yet their clothes were drenched, and would take hours to dry. Naked, they sat around against the rails, trying not to look uncomfortable. Karl felt uneasy; looking at naked women was fun, yet he was too embarrassed to enjoy it.

"I hear something," Eloise said.

Karl stood up and looked around. There was some strange noise, yet it was too distant to make out.

Then they heard it: a warhorn, blowing across the waves.

Far away, but sailing right toward them, came another dragonship, with a full sail and plying thirty oars.

"Vikings ...!" Karl shouted.

Karl's weapons and armor were tightly stowed and tied down in the hull; he'd never reach them in time. Even if he could, what good was one sword against a hundred pirates? To be captured by bloodthirsty Vikings was the worst thing he could think of ... except to be caught by them naked.

"Hide ...!" Seren shouted, but there was no place to hide.

Suddenly Seren started pulling up deck planks, and Karl realized her plan. They all pulled up planks, then crawled inside the wet hull, pulling the Seer's limp body in with them. Squeezed for room, Karl laid flat atop Seren and Eloise, skin against skin, and Rafe got in last, pulling the planks back into place as he did.

Voices shouted from the other Viking ship; Rafe slid the last plank into place just seconds before booted feet landed on their deck.

Karl panicked, yet stayed frozen, trying not to move or breathe. He didn't know if he was more frightened or embarrassed, but as he felt the boots of armed Vikings press the deck planks against his back, he clenched his teeth and squeezed down against Eloise and Seren.

Voices raised on the deck above them, sounding threatening, like a challenge. Karl couldn't understand Norwegian, but he guessed they'd been seen.

Suddenly manly voices screamed in terror. Some fell down hard upon the deck, and others ran shouting over its planks. Soon all the Vikings jumped back onto their own ship, some splashing into the cold ocean waters, fighting to away.

Long minutes passed in silence. Frightened shouts of the Vikings faded in the distance.

Finally Rafe lifted two planks and poked his head above deck.

"They're gone ...!" Rafe announced.

Rafe pushed up more planks and climbed out. Karl pushed against the planks with his back, trying not to notice he was still naked ... and laying atop two naked women.

"Stay low!" Rafe warned, peering over the rail. "They can still see us."

Karl scooted over beside Roselyn, who was pressed against the sleeping Seer, so Eloise and Seren could breathe without his weight crushing them. Then he looked back and smiled.

The hood of the black-cloaked figure manning the rudder was thrown back. The Vikings must've revealed Eric, then fled in horror, thinking they were on a death ship.

Roselyn started laughing loudly, and soon they all joined her.

Late that afternoon, their clothes were dry enough to wear. All dressed, then Eloise and Roselyn opened up their soaked chest from Castle Bristlen. It was deep with water, and they began pulling out the wet clothes that they'd packed, and hung them to dry. Karl extracted their armor and few weapons, and cleaned them as best he could, yet he had no oil to prevent them from rusting. Rafe laced the awning back up over the front of the boat, and they re-dressed the Seer and dragged him inside.

"How long do you think he'll sleep?" Karl asked.

"As long as Eric is steering, I guess," Rafe said. "He told me to take care of his body, that he wouldn't be dead, right before he cast his spell."

"What about his moonstone?" Roselyn asked. "How can we follow Eric's trail while he's asleep?"

"What's to follow?" Rafe said, nodding aft. "If the Seer's spell worked, then that's Eric."

Karl looked back at the ghostly cloak. They'd hoisted the sail shortly after the Vikings left, and then the black cloak leaned on the tiller and steered them north.

Karl cautiously approached it.

"Eric ...? Eric, is that you ...? It's Karl. Can you hear me ...?"

The cloaked figure didn't move or speak. Karl addressed it several more times before he finally quit.

Yet looking at the empty hole atop the cloak unnerved him; before leaving, Karl reached back and pulled the long hood back over its invisible head.

The Seer didn't awaken.

Eric, if it was Eric, tended to his steering silently. Pulling on the ropes in the back, he slowly turned their sail and steered masterfully. Rafe and Karl hurried to adjust the secondary lines whenever they heard the sail turn. Their ship sped northward, water splashing high from its bow.

Over the next few days, the Seer's face grew pale. His lips chapped. Eloise began using the last of their precious clean water to keep a wet cloth over his lips, and often she, Seren, or Roselyn would crawl under a blanket and sleep beside him just to keep him warm. Even Rafe seemed worried.

"No man can live asleep," Rafe said. "He needs water and food. If the Seer doesn't wake up soon, he'll die."

"What if we poured just a little water down his throat ...?" Roselyn asked.

"You'd fill his lungs and he'd drown," Rafe said. "Eloise is on the right track, keeping his mouth moist. But that can't save him."

"If I understand this rightly, then the Seer has linked himself with Eric to bring him here, just like Svenson's wise one did to summon Skaldi the Giant,"

Karl said. "Yet we don't know how to send 'Eric' back, or what effect that would have on the Seer."

"We can pray for him," Rafe said.

"Will God help one who serves the Lady?" Eloise asked.

"I don't know," Rafe said. "But what else can we do?"

Rafe led them in a long prayer, reciting Latin they all knew by heart, though none could translate. As the sun descended, the company prayed for the Seer.

Karl closed his eyes and recited as fervently as the rest of them. He'd never put much faith in praying, yet it was their only hope. He had no idea where the cloaked figure was leading them, how to make it go away, or even if he should. It could sail them north into what Rafe called the Frozen Lands and leave them there to die. Or it could sail them all the way to the Seer's 'crack in the world' and strand them there. Either way, only magic could save them; if the Seer died, so would they.

Several more days passed. The Seer grew worse. One of the women stayed with him constantly. His color faded until his skin became white as chalk.

The Seer was dying.

"Land ...!" Seren shouted the next morning. *"Land ...!"*

All stood and looked. Tall white peaks loomed ahead of them, in the distance, rising from the water.

Karl cheered, and Eloise and Roselyn hugged him excitedly.

"Wait, before you begin celebrating," Rafe warned. "It may not be what you think."

An hour later, all hopes lay dashed. The women began crying and Karl felt just as bad.

As they sailed past the 'land', all could see that the mountains of ice were small, barren, bleak islands of frozen death.

"They're not islands," Rafe said. "Sailors tell terrible stories of them: icebergs, great mountains of ice broken free and floating on the water. We're entering the Frozen Lands."

The wind grew colder, and still they sailed north. The Seer's condition worsened, and all began staying under the canvas, burning a small fire for warmth. Quickly their firewood depleted, and then they burned their empty chests and kegs. Soon they were gone, and then they burned loose deck planks just to stay warm.

They spoke little and huddled shivering under cloaks.

The next morning, all awoke to a terrible, loud banging.

Pushing out of the awning, Karl found that the cloaked figure was agitated, hammering the rail with the tiller. All turned around and saw their deaths.

Land stretched before their eyes, but like a nightmare. Tall mountains of lifeless ice, bare of tree or grass, stared ominously back at them, a portent of their future.

Empty. Bleak. Lifeless.

Karl turned to 'Eric', about to curse him, when he noticed something strange. Their sails were slack for the first time since Rafe had raised them the morning after the storm. They were floating, not sailing, relatively motionless; the cloaked figure keeping their dragonship turned so that their sails fluttered weakly, his cowl turned to face the desolate coast.

"Tide's going in ... but not for long," Rafe said, shivering, his chill breath clouding white before his face. "See those tide-marks by that huge crack, how few are left? Pretty soon it'll be ..."

The cloaked figure banged the tiller against the rail again. All looked, and suddenly the ghostly black cloak pointed at the sail, then swung its hidden arm down.

"Guess he wants us to lower the sail," Rafe shrugged.

"Do," Seren said. "Best no make spirit mad."

Karl and Rafe unlaced most of the awning, all the way to their dirt fireplace, where only a few coals smoldered. Then they turned to the lines.

Suddenly the ship came about, the sail catching and filling with south-blowing winds. Their dragonship turned to the barren, unfertile coast. Rafe and Karl chipped frost from the mast-line and began to untie it; the rope was tight and frozen, but they managed to scrape off the ice and loosen the knots. By the time the sail was finally lowered, they were rocking with the waves, almost into the surfline. They stared at the ever-rising cliffs of ice and the huge vertical crack they were sailing straight at.

"Wait a minute," Rafe said. "The sail's down, but we're picking up speed. What's going on ...?"

They were riding the surf toward land, but heading directly at the one place where there was no beach, into the tiny gap between two great cliffs of ice. Overwhelming, the colossal ice-walls dominated the frigid view, massive and still. Yet between its frozen walls they saw a watery grave in the making, where icy waters splashed as if boiling, violently swirled, and poured over rocks that could only be overborne during the tidal peak.

Karl looked back at the Seer's floating black cloak, which was wielding the rudder as if it were a mighty oar. He recognized the maneuver; from the battlements of Castle Bristlen, he'd seen Eric dock his ship in this manner, far below him in Demril Harbor, the day he'd first seen his Viking face. He had no idea why the hooded figure was steering them here, or knew of any way to stop it.

The current flowed swiftly into the narrow causeway and pulled them with it. Their dragonship cruised inside the gap and struck its choppy waters. The ship's timbers suddenly trembled; its hull shook as if it would fall apart.

"Good-bye ...!" Karl shouted to the others, clutching the side to keep from being tossed overboard.

"Don't give up yet ...!" Eloise cried, clinging to the mast with Seren. *"If that's Eric, he must know what he's doing!"*

Big 'if', Karl thought. Yet Eric was working the tiller franticly, pushing to keep them from smashing into the massive sides of the ice-walls, and moving them farther inwards.

"Where water going ...?" Seren asked, looking ahead.

"Waterfall ...!" Rafe cried. *"Hold tight ...! Everyone, hold on ...!"*

Eloise screamed as their huge dragonship tilted forward, and they heard its hull and main keel scrape against hard rocks. Vibrating, it trembled, teetered, and then abruptly fell, dragon-head first, over the falls.

They splashed into a river with a crash that sent them all tumbling. The falls had only been about eight feet high, angled so they couldn't see the river until they plunged into it.

The shallow river was made of sea-water gushing in, which pushed them away from the falls. Yet a strange roaring noise filled their ears.

The narrow river, walled by ice, emptied out into a small, splashing lake. Its surface churned and frothed, and in its center, they saw the source of the loud roaring ... and froze in terror.

In the center of the lake spun a swirling spiral of water, spinning down into darkness.

Whirlpool ...!

'Eric' pushed frantically, ghostly black cloak leaning on the shaking tiller, fighting the current, steering them to the side, against one massive ice-wall.

Their hull scraped against ice; its fatal grinding set Karl's teeth on edge. Their ship hadn't been built to withstand the punishment they were giving it; soon it'd break apart ... and they'd drown in the freezing water.

There was no other way out of this lake, no path or beach, save for swimming back up the frozen river, and climbing the waterfall, to reach the dismal coast ... where they'd die on its barren beach. Their only other escape was to sail into whirlpool, their fastest, perhaps most merciful ending.

Long hours passed. 'Eric' struggled continuously, fighting to keep them near the promethean walls as the waters swirled them repeatedly around the deadly lake's edge.

Suddenly part of the roar vanished. Karl spied the rushing river, that fed the omnivorous lake; its waters slowed, becoming almost calm as the last of the river emptied into the lake, its source cut off; the high tide had receded.

Now there was no way out ...!

Quickly the level of the lake they sailed upon began to lower, as if it were a giant well. 'Eric' fought unceasingly to keep them from the swirling, circling vortex in its center, yet the ice-walls were sloping, the pool's radius growing smaller.

"Whirlpool come …!" Seren cried.

Karl saw its center slowly move towards them. Yet 'Eric' remained silent, seemly unconcerned, and the rush of the water pushed them on as the vortex moved to cling to the spot by the wall where they'd just been.

Karl could bear it no longer, yet there wasn't anything he could do. He felt helpless, tiny compared the overpowering immenseness of the ice walls and the violent swirl of the vortex.

Suddenly the vortex vanished, replaced by a tiny crack in the ice-wall, into which their vast waters poured. A cave appeared, widening as the water rushed into it, exposing it as a black, ominous hole. The whole lake lowered, and emptied into it. Karl relaxed; when the water level reached even with the bottom of the cave's entrance, then the lake would level off.

Suddenly 'Eric' jerked the rudder about and steered their mighty dragonship straight for the growing cave. Rafe cried out, yet Eric pushed and pulled on the tiller, franticly rowing them toward the rushing current, which swept them up like a twig on a swollen stream.

As the dragonship lurched forward, they screamed and threw themselves down upon the deck. Even 'Eric', in his invisible form, swathed in the Seer's black cloak, ducked low and as flat as possible. Unstoppably they drove at the dark cave's mouth, and then they burst into its lightless interior. Their sturdy mast smashed in half as it hit the cave-mouth's roof, severing with a mighty *Crack!*, tearing up their remaining decking and breaking a gap in their wooden rail. The thick, falling mast smashed through the wood and fell overboard. Lines attached to it whipped wildly, striking and tripping them, and swiftly tautened as the mast vanished beneath the rushing waters.

Darkness consumed them. Swiftly they flowed down a long tunnel, pushed by the violent current, their hull scraping one side, then the other, as they were helplessly tossed. They flew past innumerable dark side-tunnels, opening to routes unknown, helpless to stop their ship or glimpse where the tunnels might lead.

Finally they poured out onto a sunless lake where the waters stilled, and and their boat splashed in and slowed. Several minutes later, the last of the rushing water poured in behind them, and a silence fell like the whisper of a chill grave. A strange green light shined upwards from below the water; it lit the whole cavern.

Fearing to relax, they drifted across the waters of the subterranean lake, gazing in awe at its huge ceiling, glistening colored stalactites reaching down from a natural roof, and walls of polished stone. They seemed to have come to the end of their road, yet none of them dared to speak, fearing to break the eerie silence of the fantastic underground pool.

The coals of their fire had fallen onto deck-planks; a tiny fire crackled, echoing across the silent water, flickering red shadows and glistening reflections all about. Yet no one moved to extinguish it. The rippling water cast moving shadows upon the glistening, hanging stalactites, making them seem to move.

"Dead end," Rafe whispered, and his words echoed loudly.

"Dead water," Seren corrected. "If lake fill, be long ago full. Outlet somewhere."

"Where ...?" Karl asked.

"There," Roselyn whispered, pointing over the bow.

Before them stood a wide gap in the wall, lined by giant stalactites like monstrous teeth, bathed in the green glow, yet barely visible at the edge of their red light.

Behind the stone teeth all was black.

"Another cave ...?" Eloise asked.

"No, the waterline cuts across it," Karl said. "It's ... dark, black rock."

Suddenly bubbles broke the surface behind them, followed by a deafening splash. Out of the silent lake rose a huge, horrible head, green, shaped exactly like the mythical dragon carved on their prow, save that the head alone was half the size of their whole vessel.

Shock ... Alarm ... Dragon ...!

Water splashed off of it in a sudden deluge that sent them cascading forward. Slowly 'Eric' turned the rudder, easing them straight at the black empty space between the giant stone teeth.

None moved or spoke. All had been exposed to magical horrors, yet none encompassed the appalling, abominable monstrosity hovering over them, the dreadful, ultimately-formidable monument of legend. Now they were going to die, tidbits for this odious, vile leviathan whose destructiveness, Karl perceived, could easily end the world.

Never had he felt so inferior and insignificant, watching the gargantuan dragon-head rise toward the ceiling, murderous green eyes burning like emerald coals, hungry mouth opening with a seething hiss, serpentine tongue glowing red from morbid fires within, bathing giant fangs in a bloody light to encompass their very souls. Here was Dragon, the most powerful of all beasts of legend, the symbol of kings, harbinger of evil, and guardian of the underground lake of death.

Suddenly it roared, vast and deep, shaking the walls with its deafening echo, and churning the still lake. Never since days far past memory had living mortals dared trespass its dark, watery domain.

Now they were going to die ...!

Suddenly 'Eric' dropped the tiller and moved, his empty cloak gliding forward across the deck. Fear of his ghostly form stunned them all from bewildered fright; 'Eric' pushed them aside as he flowed over the collapsed, burning awning to the very prow, reached out, and touched the black wall as the nose of their wooden dragon-prow smashed into it.

Vanishing, the black wall opened into a tunnel leaning sharply downward. The still water broke forward, tearing them with it, gushing away from the horrid vengeance of the vast guardian.

Behind them, the green dragon of the underground lake roared in frustrated anger. Flames spewed forth, filling the new tunnel, yet wrenched on the water's crest, they flew faster, steeper than before, clinging to whatever lay nearest.

Despite everything, Karl sighed in relief. The strange black wall, the mouth beneath the monstrous stone teeth, opening only at a deadman's touch, was the 'crack in the world'. Now they were racing, falling through it, plummeting blindly down a hollow shaft outside of their world, faster than any human had ever fallen before, screaming for their lives and clinging to their wrecked ship as if it were their last salvation.

Their dragonship slammed hard against rocks hidden by darkness, scraping and bouncing against both sides and the invisible bottom. Karl was amazed their ship was holding together, yet certain it couldn't take much more.

Abruptly, falling water cascaded down upon them. Then they were outside, under bright stars, flying down rapids dotted with huge black rocks, steerless; no one at the rudder.

'Eric' was gone; the Seer's black cloak had fallen empty upon the foredeck.

Instantly Rafe jumped up, pulled himself low along the broken rail, and climbed to seize the tiller. Karl moved to help him, when a sudden splash rose up from beneath a hole in the deck planks, striking him in the face. Karl hesitated, surprised as his lips registered a strange, unexpected taste to the water, sweet yet bitter. Having no time to consider it, Karl quickly pushed aside more deck planks, finding deep water beneath them, with more water rushing inside through a huge hole in their wooden hull.

"Falls ...!" Roselyn screamed.

Eloise shrieked. Under a starry sky, all around them rose hills of black rock. On the steep incline, they plummeted, racing downwards, rushing on rapids under piercingly bright stars. Another waterfall loomed before them, so ominous even the starlight beyond it seemed to fail.

Rafe leaned heavily on the tiller and steered for their lives. Their failing dragonship shook, trembled against the water's fury; Karl felt certain death had them in its grasp. Then, just as they were about to shoot over the falls, Rafe drove them crashing up onto land, skidding their mighty dragonship to a groaning halt up onto a black, sloping, rocky shore.

The sudden impact threw them all forward; their dragonship roared and scraped against the rough stone. Its mighty hull cracked almost in half, and shattered timbers and broken planks flew in every direction. Then their dragonship keeled onto one side, destroyed beyond hope of repair.

Their ship was dead, murdered at the cost of saving the company from the deadly rapids, from splashing over falls so close ahead Karl's frayed nerves might never heal.

Alive ...!

Safe on land ...!

Stranded on another world.

Slowly a muffled, pained groan rose from beneath their fallen canopy.

"Seer ...!" Eloise cried, and she climbed shakily to her feet and vanished under the collapsed awning. "He's alive! Alive!"

Slowly Karl rose and looked to the prow; the Seer was alive. They were all alive.

"Karl, the ... ground ...!" exclaimed Rafe, who had tumbled over the rail as their ship hit. "It's ... not rock! It's ... wood! Black wood!"

Incredulous, Karl turned to face him, uncomprehending his words, when he saw the solid wall past him, and looked straight up.

Ever been at the foot of a large mountain, looking up, amazed at its size? That amazement was tempered by the fact that what you saw was a mountain, supposed to be big. What Karl saw was dozens of times bigger than any mountain, yet it wasn't a mountain. It was black, not like darkness, but grayish-black, and wrinkled like bark. Karl was kneeling on the edge of its world, at the bottom, on its roots, looking out at inhumanly bright stars, up at this great trunk of a black pillar, which rose higher than Karl could see, branching off into black limbs thick enough to hold entire worlds, larger than any mountain could ever be, and topped with giant leaves.

It was a tree.

End of Book 2
of
The VIKINGS! Trilogy

Next Book in the Trilogy:

Quest for Valhalla
by Jay Palmer

ABOUT THE AUTHOR

Born in Tripler Army Medical Center, Honolulu, Hawaii, Jay Palmer works as a technical writer in the software industry in Seattle, Washington. Jay enjoys parties, reading everything in sight, woodworking, obscure board games, and riding his Kawasaki Vulcan. Jay is a knight in the SCA, frequently attends writer conferences, SciFi Conventions, and he and Karen are both avid ballroom dancers. But most of all, Jay enjoys writing.

Check out my website:

JayPalmerBooks.com

Made in the USA
Middletown, DE
14 May 2022